Black Bat Mystery

AIRSHIP 27 PRODUCTIONS

Black Bat Mystery-Volume 2

Published by Airship 27 Productions
www.airship27.com
www.airship27hangar.com

Interior llustrations © 2012 Andres Labrada
Cover illustration © 2012 Ingrid Hardy & Rob Davis

Editor: Ron Fortier
Associate Editor: John Bruening
Production and design by Rob Davis.

ISBN-13: 978-0615689500
ISBN-10: 0615689507

Printed in the United States of America

10 9 8 7 6 5 4 3 2 1

CONTENTS
VOLUME 2

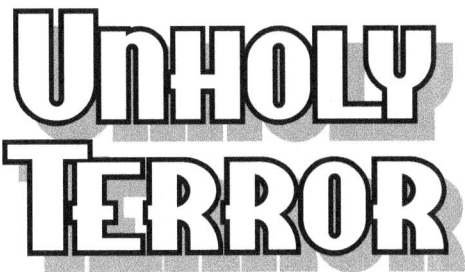

UNHOLY TERROR

A Black Bat Adventure

by
Aaron Smith

Lester Schwartz was literally shaking in his shoes. The short, scrawny, balding, bespectacled accountant stuttered as he started to speak. "B-but M-mister Cassidy, I'm n-not the kind of man who is good at things like this!"

Danton Cassidy laughed a little, but he was clearly losing his patience. "Schwartz, you silly little toad of a man, that is precisely why I've chosen you. Try to use that little brain of yours for a change! If I were to send one of my usual couriers out the front door of this building carrying that black satchel, one of the detectives who perpetually loiter around outside would surely notice him, and have him tailed all the way to his destination. You, my little friend, are the least likely to attract the attention of the law, and therefore, you must go."

Schwartz knew that the small beads of perspiration beginning to form on Cassidy's brow were an indication that the obese man was beginning to lose his temper. Schwartz nodded and picked up the black leather satchel that was on the floor of the office.

Cassidy brushed the sweat from his forehead and once again gave Schwartz his instructions. "Now remember; leave by the front door, walk at least two blocks before hailing a cab, take the cab downtown and find Jasper's Bar. Do not have the driver drop you off in front of the bar, but disembark several blocks away and walk the rest of the way. When you get to the bar, go in and give the money to the man by the pinball machine. Once he has the money, he'll give you something in return. It will be a small item, but you must take the utmost care in bringing it back to me. Is that understood? Can you remember all that?"

Too nervous to try to speak again, Schwartz simply nodded in response and began preparing to leave. His unease showed in his every movement as he carried the black satchel with him over to the closet on the opposite wall of Cassidy's office. He opened the closet door, fumbling with the knob as his hand trembled. He took his yellow raincoat down from where he had hung it upon his arrival that morning. A few minutes later, carrying the bag and clad in his raincoat and hat, Lester Schwartz was on his way down to the ground floor of the building. He had a sinking feeling in the pit of his stomach. He was perfectly content to balance

Danton Cassidy's finances, even when it involved juggling the figures into all sorts of arrangements designed to keep the authorities off the trail of Cassidy's doings. The paperwork, the calculations, and the preparation of documents were things with which Schwartz was comfortable. But this was different. To be thrust out into the streets with a case of money, more money than he made in a year, and to have to deliver it to God only knew what sort of scoundrel, was almost more than Schwartz's nervous disposition could bear. By the time he reached the ground floor, he was going over mathematical equations in his mind in a desperate attempt to not think about what he had to do.

Schwartz exited the revolving front door of the tall office building and stepped into the streets of Manhattan. It was a warm afternoon but it was raining, and the slick wetness of the sidewalks added even more to Schwartz's nervousness as he imagined himself slipping and spilling all of Cassidy's precious money all over the streets.

Schwartz managed to do what he had been ordered to do. He muddled his way through the rain-slick streets, walking several blocks from Cassidy's office, and hailed a cab. He had the driver take him to the general area of Jasper's Bar, paid his fare, leaving a small tip, and got out with his black bag of cash. He continued plodding along, the pit of nervousness in his gut growing with every footstep. He wondered who this man was, and what sort of questionable character would be waiting by that pinball machine. He would never have the chance to find out.

Schwartz was not far from his destination when another man stepped out from between two buildings and began to walk directly behind him. He failed to notice his pursuer; he was so caught up in his worries. He did not react when the stranger pressed the silencer-equipped pistol against his back and ruthlessly pulled the trigger. Schwartz's killer was no amateur and the nervous accountant died instantly. The assassin dragged Schwartz's carcass into the alley from which he had emerged moments before. The passersby on the sidewalk took no notice of the occurrence, thanks to the swift and flawless manner in which the murder had been carried out. Lester Schwartz, a small man, beneath the notice of almost everyone he had ever encountered, had passed from this world, leaving no close relations behind.

Lester Schwartz never got to meet the man by the pinball machine, but someone else did. A few short minutes after Cassidy's accountant perished, another man, carrying the same black satchel, walked casually into Jasper's Bar and strode over to the pinball machine. He met a dark-eyed, mustached man whose fedora covered his bushy gray hair. The man who had killed Lester Schwartz took a deep drag from his cigarette, ashes spilling onto his coat and dropping off onto the barroom floor as he handed the black leather bag over and received a small silk pouch in exchange. The man who had waited by the pinball machine opened the satchel just enough to peer inside at the wads of green paper, smiled, and walked away, bag in hand. The killer quickly left the bar, placing the silk bag in his vest pocket as he walked. Inside the pouch, he could feel something small and hard, but very light in weight. He was curious to know what was in the bag, but smart enough to know that satisfying his curiosity would most likely be one of the last things he would ever do. He had been ordered not to open it, and he would obey that command rather than risk his life.

Detective Lieutenant McGrath finally arrived on the scene nearly an hour after Lester Schwartz's corpse was found in the alley by a nine-year-old boy who had been playing hooky from school. The kid had sworn to Officer Sweeney that he hadn't touched the body, and that he had gone to find a policeman as soon as he saw it, and that he wouldn't even think of doing anything so disgusting, but as soon as McGrath saw the dead man, he knew the little brat had been lying. First of all, thought McGrath to himself, there was very little blood on the ground around the corpse, only a slight trickle had oozed through the man's shirt and onto his coat. When a man is shot, he usually bleeds to death, but this guy hadn't bled out. Whoever had shot him knew just where to send the bullet to stop the heart instantly. No heartbeat means less blood at the scene, but the body was in a weird tangled position, like somebody had poked it and prodded it and pushed it halfway over. Professionally trained killers don't leave bodies like that. They make the kill, take anything they need to take from the victim, and get away fast. So, McGrath figured, the kid was curious and just had to touch the body. Kids do things like that, so the detective couldn't really blame him. Who knows, he thought, the kid might grow up to be a cop with a creepy little mind like that. Secondly, the dead man's wallet was tossed by the side of the body. There was no money in it. This didn't look like the kind of man who would be out without even a few dollars on him, and the small amount of cash that a man might carry with him is not the sort of thing that would get him killed by a hired gun. So McGrath figured the kid had taken the money too. Maybe he wouldn't grow up to be a cop after all. Unfortunately, the brat had already run off, probably to brag to all his little friends about how he had touched a stiff. But he had left the wallet, which was now in McGrath's hand.

Officer Sweeney, who desperately wanted to be a detective himself, making him a royal pain at crime scenes, stood next to McGrath as the lieutenant opened the wallet. "So who was he, Lieu?" the officer begged for information.

"Name's Lester Schwartz. Dammit, Sweeney, I know that name. Why does it ring a bell? Schwartz, Schwartz, Schwartz," repeated McGrath as he tried to jog his memory.

"I don't know, Lieu. He doesn't look like the sort of fellow you'd have arrested before. He looks more like somebody's accountant," muttered Officer Sweeney.

"That's it! This little runt was Danton Cassidy's accountant!" McGrath shouted, his memory awakened by Sweeney's incidental observation.

Sweeney smiled the wide grin of a man who was much prouder of himself than the occasion called for. "Cassidy the crime boss, you mean?"

"You mean 'alleged' crime boss, Sweeney. Watch what you say out in the open. I wouldn't put it past Cassidy to sue us for slander. His accountant may have been shot dead today, but I'd bet my cigar he's got plenty of lawyers runnin' around. But maybe, if we're lucky, we can tie this poor guy's murder back to his boss somehow. Of course, you didn't just hear me say that, did you Sweeney?"

Sweeney did not reply, but merely shook his large barrel-shaped head. McGrath pulled a fresh cigar from his trench coat pocket and lit it, puffing it to life as he turned and walked away from the body, giving the signal for the coroner's assistant to take it away. Officer Sweeney followed him like a hungry puppy.

Not far away, in a small rented apartment, Colonel Klaus Reinhardt eagerly grabbed the small silk pouch from the hand of the man who had just delivered it to him. Reinhardt dismissed the man with a wave of his hand, having instilled so much fear in his underlings that words were not often needed to prompt obedience. He cupped the silk bag in his large hands, and then slowly, carefully untied the strings that secured the top of it. He pulled the bag's contents out with two fingers and finally saw the object he had been sent to New York City to gain possession of. The tiny glass vial contained what in Reinhardt's mind was a treasure, a wonderful mechanism of power and terror that, when put into use, could only serve to further the cause to which he had pledged his life.

Colonel Reinhardt was in love, in love with his rank and position. There was no woman in his life, but he was as devoted to the success of the Nazi party as Romeo was to Juliet. He was fiercely proud to be part of the Master Race and an officer in the elite S.S., and would use any means necessary to succeed in whatever task was placed before him by his superior officers. Reinhardt was a tall man, towering over nearly everyone he had ever met. His hair was closely cropped and an almost metallic gray color. It complimented his piercing black eyes and strong, square jaw. He looked like a soldier, walked like a soldier, and could kill like a soldier when he had to, but usually preferred to let his agents and other minions perform the dirtiest of tasks for him. He gave orders, they followed orders, and enemies died. It was a simple and effective equation by which Klaus Reinhardt's life was kept in perfect order.

Reinhardt clapped his hands twice. At the signal, the door opened and three men entered. They stopped directly in front of the Nazi colonel and quickly raised their arms in the Nazi salute. All three men had identical expressions on their faces; emotionless, cold, dangerous. Reinhardt held the small vial in his right hand and used his left to carefully remove the stopper. He put the stopper down on a table in front of him and picked up a chemist's dropper. With the dropper, he transferred a minuscule portion of the vial's clear liquid contents into each of three smaller vials. These new containers were tiny, small enough to be concealed almost anywhere. Once these smaller vials were occupied, Reinhardt sealed them and handed one to each of the three men before him. He then resealed the original vial, which still contained some of the liquid which had cost Lester Schwartz his life. He took the silk pouch in which he had received it from his jacket pocket, put the vial safely inside it, and then put it back. Colonel Reinhardt then gave some very specific instructions to his three agents, his powerful staccato voice snapping out the words as his men made sure not to miss any detail, no matter how small. They knew that no mistake or failure would be tolerated by Klaus Reinhardt. The three agents saluted their commander again, turned quickly, and trotted out of the room, eager to serve the Reich.

Tony Quinn stood in the private washroom just off of his law office in a Manhattan building. He finished washing and drying his hands and looked straight ahead into the mirror mounted above the sink. At first glance, he appeared to be a handsome man, but not in a movie star way. His looks were of the more rugged variety, like those of a football player or a cattle rancher. Anyone seeing him with his dark glasses on would most likely think of what a shame it was that a strong, broad-shouldered young man would have the misfortune of being blind. However, if someone were to see him without the glasses, they would have had a much different first impression. Quinn's eyes functioned perfectly or perhaps even more than perfectly. His eyes were one of his two most striking features. They were dark, piercing eyes, unlike any eyes that one was likely to encounter on a daily basis. His eyes had a strange silvery shimmer to them, the unexpected result of a double cornea transplant that had been performed in secret. The secrecy allowed the world at large to continue to believe that Tony Quinn was, in fact, a blind man. Not only did his eyes work as well as anyone's; they were far better. Somehow, the operation he had endured had enhanced his eyes, allowing him perfect vision in any amount of light, whether during the brightness of day or the shadowy darkness of night.

Quinn's other notable feature was the series of vivid scars that ran down his face on either side of his eyes. They were jagged lines, resembling the marks of a tiger's claws. He had not, however, been mauled by any beast of the jungle, but had been scarred by a beast of the city. During a trial when he was a young prodigy of a district attorney, a petty thug had taken the opportunity to throw a powerful acid in Quinn's face. The resulting damage had been twofold. Tony Quinn had been blinded, and he had been horrifically scarred. The clandestine corneal surgery had corrected the blindness, giving him sight superior to that of most men, but he had to learn to live with the scars.

Quinn turned away from the mirror and headed back into his office. As he walked, he kept reflecting on the events of the past few years of his life. Following the acid attack that had robbed him of his sight, he resigned from his district attorney's position. During his hiatus from work as an attorney, the public believed that he was adjusting to his new blindness, but in reality he was doing several much more interesting things. He underwent the secret surgery that gave him his improved vision, and he spent countless hours in training himself for a new task that he felt obligated to undertake after feeling firsthand the terrible pain that could be inflicted upon innocents by an underworld gone wild.

Using his wealth, his wits, his physical prowess, and his unique sight, Tony Quinn had pledged to wage a two-sided war against the shady criminal underbelly of New York City. In the light of day, Quinn was a by-the-book attorney, blinded by crime, but still a believer in the law and its righteousness. In the dark of night, he became the mysterious Black Bat, a masked vigilante, dressed from head to foot in a jet black costume, with a flowing cloak cascading behind him. So black was his attire that only his weird, piercing, haunting eyes could be seen by anyone who had the steel-strong nerve they would need to even dare gaze upon his terrifying form. As the Black Bat, Quinn relentlessly assaulted the criminals of the city, his twin .45 caliber automatics blazing through the shadows of dark alleys and warehouses full of contraband materials, tearing through the best laid plans of New York's most wicked crime lords, vengeful, unstoppable, deadly. Distrusted by the police and the public, feared and loathed by the criminals he pursued, and the subject of rumors and whispered legends, the Black Bat was a figure shrouded in mystery and lore.

His mind finally coming back to the present, Tony Quinn glanced around his office. Once he had regained his sight, he returned to the legal profession, this time in private practice. His office was designed specifically to give the impression that it did indeed belong to a blind lawyer. The walls were mostly bare, for what use would a sightless man have for paintings or photographs? The only adornment was the framed law school diploma on the wall, more for the reference of his clients than for himself. On his desk was an untidy heap of legal documents and other papers. Those papers in plain sight when visitors came to the office looked like they were written in Braille, with small raised dots in varying patterns. However, anyone proficient in reading Braille would have been mystified had they tried to read these legal briefs, for they were just gibberish. The Braille was there to fool the public. The real legal documents and case files were written or typed in normal English and carefully hidden in Quinn's desk drawers, to be taken out only when he was alone, or in the company of one of his few trusted confidantes and friends.

Enough reminiscing, he thought. It was time to get back down to business, and he pulled a bundle of papers from under the desk and began to lose himself in the planning of his next courtroom strategy.

Like many blind people, during the course of the months between the acid attack and the miraculous sight-restoring procedure, Tony Quinn had found that his remaining senses had grown more acute; he noticed more with his ears, nose and fingertips than he ever had when he could see. Even now, with his vision returned to him, his sharp hearing could tell him things that others would never notice. He had had a feeling that he wasn't going to get much work done this day, and his ears were now confirming that instinct. One of the most interesting things about really listening to the sounds of your surroundings, thought Quinn, was that every person makes a unique sound as they walk. Things like weight, height, general physical condition, attitude, pacing, type of clothing worn and even length of hair added to the symphony of noises that made up the sound of a person walking. A person with normal hearing, not sharpened by countless hours of disciplined drilling, would never notice all those things, but Tony Quinn could. Without conscious effort he analyzed the footsteps coming down the hall towards his office door. The clicking of high heeled shoes, the swish of a skirt, the slight rustle of long blonde hair told him that it was Carol Baldwin…and he remembered their lunch date, and cringed at the thought of the reprimanding he was about to get.

The door flew open and Carol Baldwin came storming in. She was a gorgeous woman but had an angry look on her face this time. There was no need for Quinn to pretend he couldn't see her mood written on her face, for she was one of the few people who knew he wasn't really blind. In fact, the transplanted corneas that had given him back his sight had once belonged to her now dead father, a police officer. It was Carol who had arranged and paid for the operation to restore Tony Quinn's vision, although at the time she did not expect the side effect of perfect night vision to accompany her gift.

"You have some nerve forgetting our appointment after all I've done for you, Mister Quinn!" she began to hiss at him. He knew her use of the title 'mister' indicated real anger and he decided he had better calm her down right then and there before things got any worse.

"I'll pay for lunch," he offered.

"You were already paying for lunch! You'll have to do better than that," Carol retorted.

Quinn sighed and made another attempt, "Fine. I'll let you pick the place. Any restaurant in town; it's your call."

She smirked a little, "That's better. I guess I'll forgive you. We're going to Francini's."

With that, Tony Quinn donned his jacket and grabbed his white cane. The cane, of course, was there to add to the illusion of his blindness. He and Carol strolled out of the office, arm in arm, and he shook his head. Although he had plenty of money, most of it was carefully budgeted to allow him to continue his rather expensive nocturnal activities as the Black Bat, and he knew that Francini's was going to cost him a nice chunk of change.

"I'll pay for lunch," he offered.

Danton Cassidy was livid; his face crimson with anger. His hands trembled as rage shook his entire massive body. He had just received word of Lester Schwartz's death. It was not grief for his accountant that had him so enraged, but the idea that his prize, the object he had sent Schwartz to procure, had been taken by someone else.

"Get me Mister Speck!" he bellowed to one of his assistants, "Get him here now!"

When Danton Cassidy was angry, his men knew better than to keep him waiting, and forty-five minutes later Willard Speck waltzed into Cassidy's office. Speck was an odd looking fellow, and his look was intentional. Strip away the intentional oddities of his look, and you would be left with a painfully average man. Speck's natural looks were so mundane that no one would give him a second glance under most circumstances. He had average looks, was of average size and build and, unadorned, nothing about him was anything other than average. To make up for his mediocrity of appearance, Speck made sure he stood out. He always wore a black suit, composed of a black jacket, black vest, black shirt, and black pants. In contrast to the black, he wore a white fedora, white bow tie, white gloves, and white shoes. The stark difference between the black and white made him resemble a walking domino. He had a long thin black moustache and often wore dark glasses when outdoors. He also had the peculiar habit of keeping a long cigarette holder dangling from his mouth most of the time, but it was perpetually empty, as Speck did not smoke.

Willard Speck was a private investigator, but had a somewhat different clientele than most PIs. Speck worked for men like Danton Cassidy; the cream of the crop of the underworld. Speck was discreet, smart, and sneaky. He worked quickly and he always got the information his clients wanted.

"Sit down, Mr. Speck," commanded Danton Cassidy, "As you have doubtlessly heard by now, my personal accountant, Lester Schwartz, was found dead in an alley this afternoon. What you may not know is that he was on an errand for me. I had sent him to an establishment called Jasper's Bar to make a pickup for me. He was to rendezvous with a man who was supposed to be waiting by a pinball machine. I suspect that whoever killed Schwartz may have met this man instead, and used my money to gain possession of an item that was by now supposed to be in my hands. I want you to go to this bar and find out whatever information you can. Report back to me as soon as possible."

Cassidy pulled a thick wad of bills from his desk drawer, handed some of the money to Willard Speck, and returned to what he had been doing.

Speck left quickly and quietly, having no intention of making Cassidy wait any longer than he had to.

Impressively, it took less than an hour for Speck to make it back to Cassidy's office. Less impressively, he had little to report, but Cassidy had expected as much.

"Nothing, Mr. Cassidy, nothing at all, except for one tiny clue and it's not a clue that you're going to like. Whoever took your item made sure to attract as little attention as possible. The bartender remembered the guy who had been waiting by the pinball machine, but he had no recollection at all of the man who came to meet him there. Whoever this guy was, he was good. But somebody did spill some cigarette ash on the floor in the spot where the meeting probably took place. I pride myself on remembering the scents of different cigarettes; it comes in handy in my line of work, so I took a whiff. Those ashes came from a German-made cigarette, not sold anywhere in the States or most of Europe either. I'd say that gives you about a 90% chance this guy was really a German, which might mean spy these days!" reported Willard Speck before sticking the empty cigarette holder back between his lips and exiting the room.

As he walked out, Speck could hear Danton Cassidy's fist slamming down on the desk with a powerful thud. Cassidy hated Nazis. Although he had lived in New York for most of his life, Cassidy had been born in Europe and still had plenty of relatives there, so he had a personal interest in the war that raged overseas. His last name, Cassidy, had come from his Irish father. His mother was French, and his first name, Danton, was taken from a prominent figure in the French revolution. He most certainly did not want Nazis meddling in his affairs, and it made him almost sick to his stomach to imagine what they might do with the contents of the little glass vial that should have been his. He had had no intention of ever using it on people. He just wanted to scare his rivals into submission after giving a little demonstration on a stray dog or some other unfortunate but inconsequential animal. Danton Cassidy may have been a thief, a scoundrel, a blackmailer, an extortionist, and a murderer by proxy (he had long since given up getting his own hands dirty with the actual killing), but he sure as hell was no Nazi.

Lieutenant McGrath had been summoned to the commissioner's office. He stood on the steps outside, taking one long last drag on his cigar. The commissioner made him a little uneasy, although he would never let it show. He had his tough-as-nails reputation to protect after all. He stepped on the little butt that was left of the cigar and went inside. The secretary sent him right in and he found Commissioner Jerome Warner standing there, staring out his office window. Warner turned to face McGrath.

The commissioner spoke, and by the tone of his voice McGrath could tell he had a lot on his mind. Warner was a strong-willed man and when he made up his mind about something, it was tough to argue. "Well, McGrath, Captain Henderson seems to think we ought to charge Danton Cassidy in the murder of this Schwartz fellow. It's about time we caught a break in going after that scum!"

McGrath nearly stuttered as he responded, "We can't do that, Sir! I've just begun my investigation. There's no evidence of anything yet!"

Commissioner Warner looked shocked that the detective lieutenant would dare try to debate the matter, "Captain Henderson thinks it could work. Schwartz worked for Cassidy. Schwartz was killed by a professional. It's not much of a stretch to assume that Schwartz had something on Cassidy and had become a threat that had to be done away with. We can make this stick, Lieutenant!"

McGrath's anger was rising now, and he was on the verge of forgetting by how much Warner outranked him. "Henderson is a pompous idiot! The whole case will be blown if we pursue this with no hard facts! Just give me a few days, Commissioner. I'll find something!"

The commissioner shook his head and gave McGrath a lot less than a few days. "You have twenty-four hours, McGrath. Then I let Henderson have his way."

With that, Detective Lieutenant McGrath turned around and stormed out of the commissioner's office.

Tony Quinn and Carol Baldwin had had a delightful lunch. Francini's was well worth the huge bite it had taken out of Quinn's wallet. With a full stomach and a bit of lipstick on his collar, he strolled, white cane tapping along the floor, back to his law office. He sat down behind his desk, humming to himself, and was about to dive headfirst back into his work, when a knock resounded on the door.

"Come in. It's open," he said, loudly enough to be heard through the door without shouting. The door opened and Quinn immediately recognized the man who entered, but could obviously not let on that he knew him by sight. He did, however, decide to have a bit of fun with his visitor. "Good afternoon, Lieutenant McGrath," said Quinn, "What can I do for you today?"

McGrath had convinced himself months ago that Quinn was faking his blindness. He was correct of course, but Quinn would never let him know that. That would only add fuel to the detective's other suspicions about Quinn, and those suspicions were, in some ways, far more serious business.

"For a blind man," said McGrath sarcastically, "you sure recognized me right away, Quinn!"

"Of course I did," shot back Tony Quinn, with a mischievous smirk, "One doesn't have to see to recognize the stench of those cheap cigars you're always puffing on."

Ignoring Quinn's attempt at humor, McGrath got right down to business, "You know I don't like you, Quinn. I don't trust you and I haven't stopped believing that you've got some connection to that maniac, the Black Bat! However, I'll admit this much; you know how to get things done. I know you've still got connections down at the D.A.'s office, and I need you to keep an eye on a certain situation for me."

McGrath then proceeded to fill the young attorney in on the whole story of the discovery of Lester Schwartz's body, the commissioner's theory about Danton Cassidy's involvement, and the department's plans to (McGrath was assuming) frame Cassidy for the killing. Quinn could tell that McGrath was desperate for some help. He must have been if he would come to Quinn, of all people, in a situation like this. Quinn knew though, that despite the fact that McGrath was annoying, he believed in doing the right thing no matter what. Tony Quinn decided right then and there that he would look into the whole matter, but he would do most of the looking not as a supposedly blind young lawyer, but as The Black Bat.

McGrath excused himself and left the building. Once the detective was gone, Quinn finished up a few tasks and got ready to head home for the evening. He grabbed his hat and coat and ever-present cane and made his way to the first floor. His car was waiting outside, with Silk Kirby in the driver's seat. Kirby was one of Tony Quinn's few confidantes. During the day, he served as Quinn's chauffeur and valet. By night, Silk Kirby was one of the Black Bat's trusted aides. Formerly a two-bit con artist, Kirby now used his street smarts and underworld connections to help the Black Bat in his assault on the criminal elements of the city.

Kirby drove quickly and the car, with its two passengers, soon arrived at Quinn's home. It was a spacious, expensive house outside the confines of the busy streets of Manhattan, but still within the city limits; a perfect residence for a man of Tony Quinn's unusual lifestyle. Driving through a hidden entrance in the rear of the property that led to a series of tunnels below the ground, Silk Kirby drove the car into the house's underground garage. They got out and Quinn quickly discarded his white cane and took off his dark glasses. There was no need to feign blindness here in his base of operations. Kirby parked Quinn's regular car next to his other vehicle, a black coupe. It was an ugly old car, dilapidated so that it could blend in with its surroundings when used by the Black Bat. When Kirby and Quinn arrived, another man rolled out from under the black coupe. He was a giant of a man, well over six feet tall, resembling a circus strongman. This was Butch O'Leary, the Black Bat's other confidante and helper. Like Kirby, O'Leary had once been a criminal, a petty thug, but Tony Quinn had seen some goodness in him and given him a second chance, a chance to join his mission. Now O'Leary did whatever Quinn asked of him, whether it was to maintain his cars or shake down a stool pigeon for information needed for one of his cases as the Bat.

"Afternoon, Boss, "O'Leary greeted Quinn, "I've got this old heap purring like a well-fed kitten. She should be ready for you whenever you need her. Will you be going out tonight?"

"I will," answered Quinn, "I need some info on this Schwartz case. I'll fill you guys in over dinner. Then I'm leaving for the night. I intend to pay a visit to Mr. Danton Cassidy."

Night fell on the city. It was a dark night, no moon visible. The coupe was parked on a dim, lightless side street. The Black Bat had parked it there and stealthily traveled to his destination. Covered almost completely in black, he was impossible to spot in the darkness. His flowing black cloak trailed behind him. Only his two piercing eyes showed through the narrow slits in his mask. Using his well-honed muscles, he had scaled the outer walls of the apartment building where his prey lived. His gamble had paid off and the window was unlocked. He slipped noiselessly inside.

Sometimes being able to see in the dark was not the most pleasant thing. A man whose eyes can cut through the blackest shadows can often learn things that men were not meant to know. For example, the Black Bat now knew that Danton Cassidy drooled in his sleep. It was not a pretty sight.

Cassidy lay snoring. The obese crime lord was in a deep slumber. Next to him lay a young woman. She was pretty; a gorgeous redhead, far too attractive to have voluntarily entered Cassidy's bed. The Bat figured she had either been paid to sleep with him, or been intimidated into it with threats of bodily harm. Either way, he felt sorry for her, but knew that she could not have had a heart of gold to be associating with him to begin with.

"Wake up, you two, "he hissed in the weird altered voice he adopted when in his guise as the nocturnal avenger.

Cassidy and the woman both sat straight up. Cassidy's chubby fingers fumbled and switched on the bedside lamp. He gasped as he saw the Black Bat perched just inside the window. The girl began to open her mouth to scream, but the Bat held up a gloved hand in a gesture to keep silent.

"Don't even think about screaming. Get up, grab your clothes and get out. Cassidy, don't move. Keep your filthy hands where I can see them. We need to have a little chat."

The girl did as she was told. She was gone within thirty seconds. Cassidy glowered at the Bat, barely keeping his rage in check, but wisely not making any sudden moves. The Black Bat waited until the girl had left the room, and then pulled his two guns from his belt, one in each hand, pointing them straight at the fat criminal in the bed. He began to speak again.

"You're a man of resources, Cassidy. You know how to get information. By now you know that the police plan to pin your accountant's murder on you. But some of them aren't so sure you're to be held responsible. I want to know everything you know, and I want to know it now! Start talking!"

Danton Cassidy was a large man, an intimidating man, a frightening hulk of a mobster, but only when staring down his own minions, the weak men with whom he intentionally surrounded himself. Now confronted by the glowering, threatening mass of moving shadow that was the Black Bat, Cassidy crumbled, spilled his guts, and told the Bat everything.

He rambled on about striking a deal with a less than ethical chemist named Crandall. The money hungry scientist had managed to develop a certain liquid substance, a fast acting poison that not only killed its victims, but did so in a most dramatic and grotesque manner. Knowing that someone somewhere would be willing to pay a lot of money for such a monstrous creation, Professor Crandall had let word leak out into the underworld about his vile accomplishment. He heard from a few interested parties, but Danton Cassidy had offered the most. So a deal was struck, a price agreed upon, and Crandall put some of his liquid horror in a little glass vial and went to Jasper's Bar where he waited at the pinball machine. Cassidy told the Bat how he had assigned the task of meeting Crandall to his accountant, the ill-fated Lester Schwartz. He begged the Bat to believe him when he claimed innocence in the matter of Schwartz's death. He told the Bat about sending the investigator, Willard Speck, to the scene of the rendezvous after learning that Schwartz was dead. He revealed everything, telling his black-clad visitor about the German cigarette that Speck had found at the scene. After he had told the Bat the whole story, all the while repeating that he had not ordered Lester Schwartz killed,

Cassidy sat back against his silk pillows, looked straight at the Black Bat, and made a request.

"Get them for me. Get them for the people of this city. Get them for the people of the world. Those German goons are going to take that poison and wreak havoc and mayhem all over the place. They'll kill thousands! Look, Bat, I was just going to use that stuff as a means of intimidation. That's all, I swear it! Even if it was more than that that I was planning, the things I deal in here in Manhattan are small potatoes compared to what's happening in Europe right now. I've got family over there. I want nothing to do with those Germans! Go get them and take that stuff and destroy it! And blow those lousy Krauts away while you're at it!"

Danton Cassidy had gotten so worked up that he had clenched his eyes shut as he growled out his little speech about the Germans. When he opened his eyes again, he was staring at an empty open window, the warm night air moving the curtains. The Black Bat had vanished into the night.

Sister Mary Eugenia didn't consider pride to be a sin, at least not when it was well-deserved pride. One must be able to tell when she had had her turn to clean the church, she thought. She did a much more thorough job of dusting the pews and sweeping out the confessionals than the other sisters ever did. She had been a nun for over twenty years and had proven her devotion to God's work many times over. So there was nothing wrong with taking a little pride in her excellent abilities. Maybe she was even entitled to an occasional reward, she thought to herself as she snuck a little sip of the communion wine. Why not? It wasn't as thought the priests measured how much was left in the bottle after each service. Who would know except her and the Lord? Surely He wouldn't mind. After her little break, Sister Mary Eugenia picked up her broom and resumed her work. She sang a little hymn to herself as she continued to tidy the place up.

A few minutes went by and she decided to step out for a smoke. She knew it wasn't considered proper for a nun to smoke and she would never dream of actually doing it inside the church, but like the wine sampling, she didn't see any real harm in it. So she stepped out onto the front steps of the cathedral and lit up. The air was warm and the dark sky was somewhat cloudy. She took a deep drag on her cigarette and watched the smoke rise upwards as she exhaled it through her long pointed nose.

She finished her cigarette, tossed the butt on the sidewalk, and turned to walk back inside the cathedral. As she took her first steps towards the door, she began to feel a strange tingling sensation in her hands. She started to feel a slight dizziness. She reentered the church, sat down on one of the pews she had dusted only moments before, and held her hands up in the dim midnight light of the room. She gasped as she saw the slow but steady trickling of blood that had begun to seep through the flesh on her palms. Her Catholic education flashed through her mind and she made an immediate mental association with the phenomenon known as Stigmata, an event that sometimes occurred, at least according to lore and legend, and seemed to mimic the wounds suffered by Christ on the cross. Stunned by this unexpected occurrence, the middle-aged nun simply sat there, shocked, feeling dizzier and more confused with every passing second.

In another part of town, Captain Ted Henderson sat in the otherwise empty police precinct. It was late, and only a few officers were on duty at this time of night. Most of them were out of the office now, either roaming the streets in their patrol cars or walking the beat. Henderson should have been home now, asleep, as his scheduled shift had long since ended, but he couldn't sleep, so he sat there with a heap of unnoticed paperwork in front of him, pondering the question of how to link Danton Cassidy to the murder of Lester Schwartz. This could be a big one, he thought to himself. Taking Cassidy down could cause his whole operation to collapse, and the resulting chain reaction was sure to earn the police captain a medal and maybe even a shot at becoming the next commissioner if that stubborn old goat Warner ever retired. Henderson lifted his coffee mug to his lips and took one final big sip, finishing off the cup. He was going to get up and pour himself another, so he put the cup down on the desk. As his hand released the coffee mug, he was startled to see a vivid red stain on the mug's porcelain exterior. Then Captain Henderson's head began to spin.

Colonel Klaus Reinhardt waited in great anticipation. His great experiment was underway, and he knew that in the morning the New York papers might bring news of how well it had gone. If successful in his mission, Reinhardt was about to bring a little taste of terror to the people of this city, and prove the worth of a new weapon which could bring a much bigger dose of horror to his enemies in Europe. A short time before, Reinhardt's three lieutenants had reported back to him. Each had returned their small glass vials, now empty. Each reported having successfully carried out his assignment. One vial had been emptied in the communion wine of one of the city's churches. The second had been used to contaminate the coffee of one of the city's police precincts. The third target would be the press. Three targets, each an essential part of the web of activities that helped to maintain the comfort and routine of the people of one of the world's most densely populated cities. The church gave faith and comfort. The police gave protection and confidence in justice. The press provided the flow of information on which the people relied. Now these German saboteurs, led by Colonel Reinhardt, would strike a small but effective blow against each of these establishments, setting off a pattern of fear that would shake the foundations of the lives of all New Yorkers. When the Fuhrer saw the reports of this, he would surely agree to use Reinhardt's deadly serum in the bigger conflict that was raging throughout Europe even as Reinhardt sat waiting in the small Manhattan apartment that has become his stateside hideout.

At the same moment, in his office at the Manhattan Tribune, Senior Editor Herman Edwards died. The malicious liquid that had been clandestinely added to his evening martini had run its course. When the night watchman made his rounds, he would find the lifeless corpse of Edwards lying on a blood soaked carpet next to his desk. He would summon the police, and the sudden gruesome death of the editor would make the front page of the morning edition.

The Black Bat had made his way back to the Tony Quinn residence after finishing his questioning of Danton Cassidy. He left his black coupe in the usual place and entered his underground lair. Walking in, he found Silk Kirby and Butch O'Leary playing cards and smoking, several empty beer bottles on the table. The Bat removed his hat and mask, revealing the ruggedly handsome, but noticeably scarred face of Tony Quinn. Electing to skip the greetings and pleasantries, he launched a question at his assistants, "Have either of you ever heard of a PI named Speck?"

Silk Kirby was the first to reply. "Sure, Boss, Willard Speck is a strange little guy, a smart one, and sneaky. He works for Cassidy sometimes. I've met him a few times over the years. He's an odd fellow. He sucks on a cigarette holder with no cigarette in it, and dresses in this crazy black and white getup all the time. Why? What's Speck got to do with all this? He didn't kill that accountant, did he? He doesn't seem like a killer to me."

"I don't think he's our murderer either," replied Tony Quinn, "but I do think he knows more than just what he told Cassidy. If this Speck is as good at finding things out as people say he is I'd be willing to bet he knows more about these German spies than he's let on. He might even know how to find them. We need to do whatever it takes to find that information." He pointed at Kirby and O'Leary as he gave his orders, "After you drop me off at the office in the morning, I want you both to go and find Willard Speck. Check any place where his kind might spend the day. When you find him,

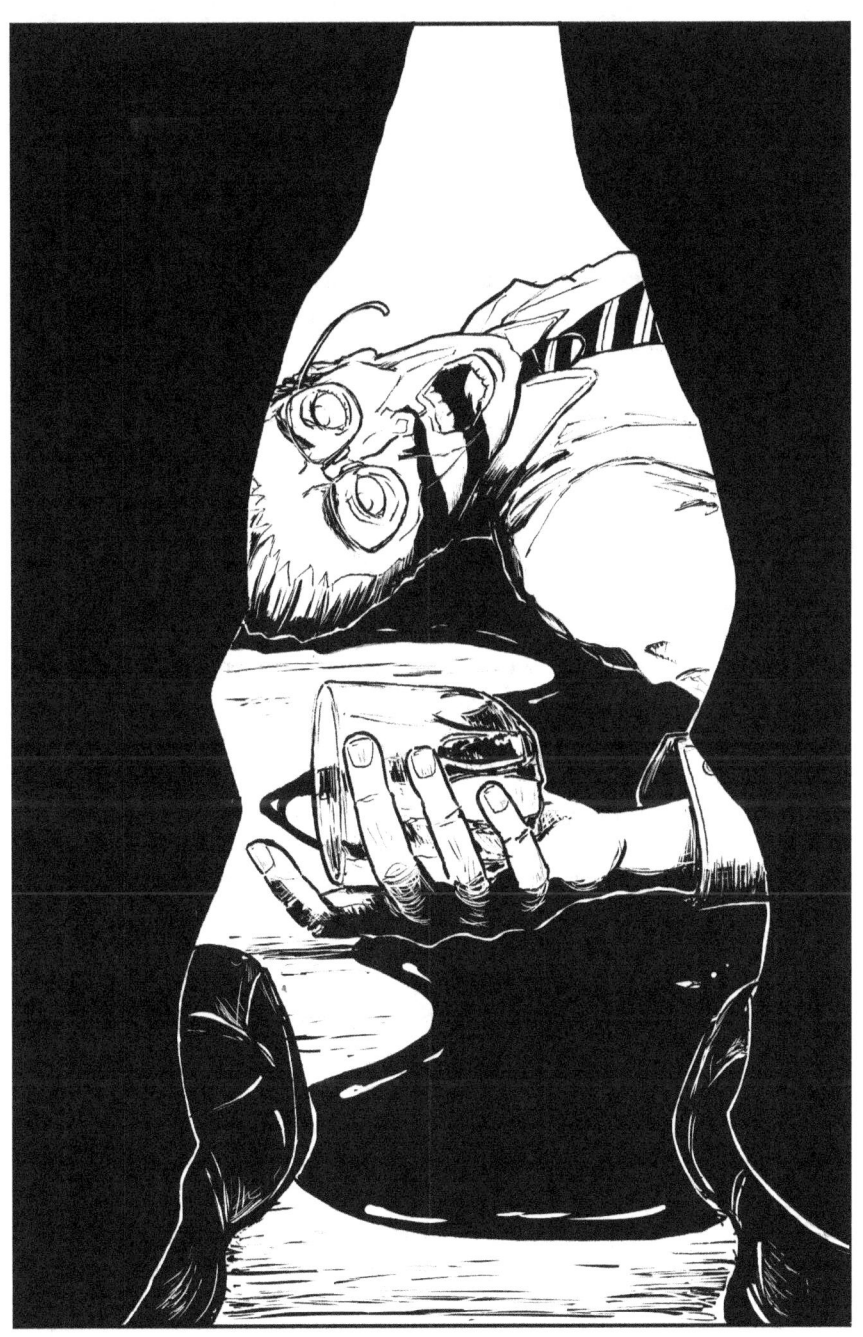

"…the night watchman….would find the lifeless corpse…"

do whatever it takes to make him talk. Silk, try your smooth talking first; try to gain his confidence and see if he spills anything. If that doesn't work, set Butch loose on him. Don't pull any punches, at least not too much. You don't want to kill him, but if a little pain will help, use it!"

Detective Lieutenant McGrath was having one hell of a bad morning. He didn't know where to start. Officer Sweeney, always punctual, had arrived at the stationhouse early and discovered Captain Henderson's body. Sweeney called McGrath immediately; waking him out of a dream about a girl he had met years before, in a little bar in Detroit, where he had been on the force before coming to New York. He hated to have such a pleasant dream cut short, but forgot all about it as soon as he was awake enough to understand Sweeney's panicked words on the other end of the line. McGrath was furious now. He may not have liked Henderson very much, but Henderson was a cop. At the moment, it wasn't clear exactly how the police captain had died. All McGrath had seen so far was a body and a lot of spilled blood, but no obvious wound from which the blood had leaked. He didn't want to make any quick assumptions, so he'd have to wait for the coroner to do his job, but if he found out that someone had murdered Henderson, there'd be hell to pay.

As he was jotting down notes and drawing himself a little diagram of the horrific scene, a young officer named O'Toole came running in to tell him that Commissioner Warner wanted him at the Manhattan Tribune building as soon as possible. Apparently, there had been another death, almost exactly like this one.

By noon, McGrath was exhausted. He had now been to all three scenes; the police precinct, the newspaper building, and the church. The three bodies were all the same. The captain, the editor, and the nun were all found dead, just lying there, most of the blood in their bodies now on the outside, staining the floors of the respective scenes. It was an ugly sight. McGrath, being a veteran detective, was used to this sort of thing, but even he had a bit of a queasy feeling in the pit of his gut. Poor Officer Sweeney had had to be ordered to go home for the day. He had gotten violently ill when he saw the crimson pools running under and between the church pews.

McGrath still didn't know where to start. The commissioner was calling him at every chance to demand that he make progress of some kind, the coroner couldn't make heads or tails of the cause of death, and to make matter even worse for the poor lieutenant, the reporters were starting to arrive in a steady stream and follow him around. One had even tried to question him when he stopped to use the bathroom.

Despite the confusion and chaos of the day, McGrath managed to keep his mind clear and continually pondered the weird events of the previous night. Three people dead with no explanation yet. Normally, his first thought would have been to wonder if the Black Bat was somehow responsible for all this, but that couldn't be the case, McGrath had told himself. While the Bat certainly had never hesitated to make bullet-riddled corpses out of thugs and thieves, he was certainly no cop killer, and it was even more inconceivable that he would slay a nun. So McGrath had to put that possibility aside and look elsewhere for a solution to the mystery.

At the same time as McGrath was trying his best to deal with the circumstances surrounding the sudden death of Henderson, Edwards, and Sister May Eugenia, Tony Quinn was in his office, behind his closed door where he needn't hide his ability to see, reading the morning paper's accounts of the mystery. He slammed his fist down and crumpled the paper. He was angry; he was horrified at what he was reading. The deadly serum that Cassidy had told him about must have already been put to use, he reasoned. According to the papers and according to his sources at the DA's office, which he had already called, the coroner had found no obvious wounds on the bodies, and the tremendous blood loss matched the symptoms of no known disease. Quinn saw no other explanation but that the Germans had struck. This meant he had failed, he thought. The Black Bat had been too slow. He had to figure out what to do before things got even worse. If he had the information he needed, specifically the whereabouts of the German infiltrators, he would put on his shadowy disguise and swoop down upon them with no mercy at all. But he couldn't do that. Manhattan was a big place and there was no way of knowing where these saboteurs might be secreted away. He would have to wait, hoping that Silk Kirby and Butch O'Leary would come through as they had many times in the past, and bring him an address.

Silk Kirby had taken Quinn's car after dropping him off at the law office and spent the morning driving around town with Butch O'Leary at his side. The two of them had checked out almost a dozen known underworld hangouts when they finally managed to locate Willard Speck. He had been spending a few hours in a seedy joint called Callahan's, downing shots and spending a bit of the money he had been paid by Danton Cassidy for the information about the pinball machine and the German cigarette. He was already half in the bag by the time Kirby walked in and recognized him. O'Leary had stayed outside on Kirby's advice, but was ready to join the fun at a moment's notice.

Inside, the place was pretty busy for so early in the day. Silk stepped up to the bar and took the stool next to Speck. "I'd ask for a light, but I know that cigarette holder's just your idea of a nutty decoration, Speck," he joked as he sat. Willard Speck glanced to his side and held out his hand in greeting.

"Silk Kirby, what brings you here? Word is you've gone straight or some other such nonsense. I didn't think it was true. That would be a terrible waste of a perfectly fine con-man!"

"Just layin' low for a while, Willie," answered Kirby, "Waiting for the right time to make a smashing comeback; waiting for the money to be right."

"And what makes now the time?" asked Speck.

"That's what the word in some corners is, Willie," Kirby replied. "I heard you might be holdin' some info I could use. What do you say we take a walk outside and talk about it? I don't trust all the ears in here."

Speck tossed a few bills down on the bar and the two got up and casually went out the front door. They ducked into an alley between the bar and the next building and stood face to face. They were almost exactly the same size; average height, both slender, but not rail thin. Kirby took out a cigarette and lit it. Speck had the ever-present empty cigarette holder dangling in his mouth.

"Tell me about the Germans, Willie," Kirby began.

Kirby could tell by the sound that was starting to come from Speck's mouth that he had just made the PI nervous. It was the sound of that silly cigarette holder clicking against his teeth, a nervous habit that Speck had had for at least as long as Kirby had been an acquaintance of his.

"Germans? I'm afraid I don't know what you mean, Silk."

Under most circumstances, Silk Kirby would have played the game a little longer. He had been an excellent con artist when he made his living that way and he was still a smooth talker, hence his nickname. But he knew that Quinn was counting on him to get the information as quickly as possible, and he would not let his boss down. He lifted his fingers to his lips and let loose a long, shrill whistle, a signal which was about to bring some serious pain into Willard Speck's world. The black and white clad private eye should not have played dumb when Kirby questioned him. Now it was too late.

At the sound of Kirby's high-pitched whistle, Butch O'Leary came bounding into the alleyway at full speed. He didn't hesitate, didn't stop to see what the situation was. As if he and Kirby had worked out a plan in advance, O'Leary grabbed Willard Speck by the jacket collar, lifted him several feet off the ground, and slammed his lean body into the brick wall with a dull, painful sounding thud!

"Couldn't do this the easy way, could we?" bellowed the giant ex-thug's loud, booming voice. He must have sounded like terrible thunder to the sly investigator, who did not like to engage in violence.

Speck let out a low moaning sound as he shuddered, stunned by the sudden force of the wall colliding with his back and shoulders. "What do you want?" he begged of O'Leary, fearing more brutality.

"An address, you idiot!" was Butch O'Leary's thunderous response. With that, just to make certain that Speck took him seriously, the huge brute swung his large fist into Speck's stomach with great force. This sent the empty cigarette holder shooting forth from Speck's lips like a bullet, to clatter to the ground. Then he let the groaning, anguished PI drop to the ground. Speck lay sprawled on the dirty asphalt for a moment before struggling to his knees. He lifted a hand, bruised from the fall, and took a pencil from his pocket. Silk Kirby handed the battered Speck a book of matches on which to write. A moment later, Kirby and O'Leary left the alleyway with an address in hand, a prize to be given to the Black Bat, and left a quivering, beaten Willard Speck writhing in pain and holding his stomach.

Kirby and O'Leary dropped by Quinn's law office after their brutal interrogation of Speck. They picked Quinn up and headed back to his residence on the outskirts of town. Quinn was pleased, as expected, with his two assistants' success in getting the needed address. They ate, and as night began to descend on the city, Tony Quinn began preparing for a night out as the Black Bat. He went through his daily exercise routine, straining his muscles to their limits as he had to be sure to remain in peak physical condition. The life of a nocturnal vigilante was a strenuous one. After his workout, he went through the procedure of donning his evening attire; black suit, black shoes, black gloves, black cape, the belt that hung about his waist to hold his two .45's and an assortment of other tools and implements of his mysterious nighttime profession, a black mask that covered all but his eyes, and lastly, a black hat. Thus dressed, he got into his black coupe, built and adjusted for speed and maneuverability rather than for looks, and sped off into the darkness of evening.

Willard Speck, meanwhile, was up to a bit of revenge. He hadn't believed Silk Kirby's claim of having not gone straight. He hadn't believed it at all. He knew, having heard it through the underworld grapevine that Kirby now worked as driver and personal aide to the attorney Tony Quinn. Quinn was certainly not known as a friend to the criminals of the city. In fact, it was even rumored that Quinn personally knew the Black Bat. Speck had given a certain address to Silk Kirby. Kirby worked for Quinn. Quinn might know the Black Bat. Willard Speck was perfectly capable of putting two and two and two together. He suspected that the address might be given to the Bat.

Speck made his way to a telephone shortly after scraping himself off the ground where Butch O'Leary's savage fists had left him. He put in a quick anonymous call to the police department, and told them to keep an eye on a certain address. Then he sat down, nursed his wounds, and smiled a twisted Judas smile.

The Black Bat's coupe roared down the dark road that led away from the residence of Tony Quinn. Part of the entire planning behind his life as the masked avenger was the location of the house in relation to the more closely cramped inner part of the city. The Quinn house was close enough to make travel into the city quick and easy, but secluded enough to almost certainly assure that no one would ever accidentally see the Bat's car leaving the area on its way to the thickly populated streets of Manhattan.

After being handed the matchbook by Kirby, The Black Bat had committed the address to memory and was heading there now. He was determined to put an end to the reign of terror that had begun the previous night when the deadly Stigmata serum had been put into play by the German spies. He refused to even consider that he might allow another human being to perish because he did not act fast enough.

Lieutenant McGrath was, by this point in the evening, exhausted. He sat at his desk drinking his eleventh cup of coffee of the day. That was far more than he usually drank, but it was all that was keeping him functional now. Of course he had made certain that the precinct's entire supply of coffee had been discarded and replaced before any officer drank any. Henderson's death while drinking coffee had convinced him to do that, even though they were still not certain that it was indeed poison that had slain the police captain. When the anonymous tip came in about the possible appearance of the Black Bat that night, McGrath had desperately wanted to go to the scene, but he knew he would just be getting in the way in his overtired state. He sent five of his best men to the building mentioned in the phone call. They were given strict orders to stay out of sight but keep their eyes wide open and try their best to not let anyone, no matter how well concealed, slip past them. McGrath knew that they were already on the scene. Doing everything he could to stay awake, he sat by the phone waiting for word from his officers.

In his small rented apartment, Colonel Klaus Reinhardt and his three lieutenants sat eating dinner. Reinhardt enjoyed cooking for his men. There was something about going through the exacting routine of measuring ingredients, pouring things together, timing the whole procedure, and arranging the components of a dish that seemed to help him think, to concentrate, similar in a way to the discipline that was needed when one was preparing explosives. He had spent the day reading the local papers and listening to the radio news reports of the panic that had ensued after the three mysterious deaths of the night before. The press and the public did not seem to know what to make of these frightening developments and they feared that worse terrors were yet to come. Now, he placed the meal on the table in front of his men and sat down with them to eat. He had sent word to his superiors in Europe that the first test of the newly acquired serum of death had been successful. Now he had to await a response and his next orders. What would they have him do next, he thought? Return home and put the liquid weapon into use in the war there, or subject it to further tests here in the United States? He hoped it would be the former, as he wanted to get back to his duties in Europe as quickly as possible. It was a glorious war being fought for the Third Reich's rightful dominion over the world. He'd have hated to miss too much of it.

The Black Bat, as per his usual method of operating, had parked his car several blocks from his destination and used his skills and abilities to move, mostly unseen, towards the place where his mission would bring him. The night, the shadows, and the very darkness itself were his allies, and he knew how to use them to his advantage. Trial and error had taught him the skills needed to hide in the shadows and stalk his prey like the deadliest nocturnal beasts of any forest or jungle. The only real difference was that the Black Bat's home was a jungle of concrete, brick and steel instead of grasses and trees. He darted confidently from shadow to shadow, avoiding the glare of the evenly spaced streetlights, clinging to walls and speeding through the darkness. He was good at what he did. He had to be. Any man foolish enough to attempt such a thing without mastering it would not have survived for very long.

The Black Bat did not approach his destination from the front door like a normal man going about normal mundane business. He understood the layout of the streets and could figure out which building was which without having to look for numbered signs on doors. He was already aware that there were several police officers in the immediate vicinity. Apparently he was expected, but he did not intend to be spotted by them. He would evade their sight and go straight to his intended targets; the German spies who were supposedly holed up in one of these cheap apartments.

He found the right building, made his way to the rear wall of the structure, pulled a length of rope with a small, sharp hook on the end of it from his belt, threw back his arm and sent the hooked end flying up, up, up to the roof of the apartment building. It made only a small clinking noise as it connected, sinking into the masonry just enough to catch, just enough to bear his weight as he began to ascend, pulling himself upwards with his strong arms as his feet did a spider-like waltz up the brick-faced wall. He knew that buildings of this type almost invariably had a roof entrance. He would use this door to make his way inside, undetected. Once in, all he had to do was find the right apartment, and send the murderers to the afterlife they so deserved.

As he climbed, he glanced down at the alley below, just to make certain that he was indeed alone. But he was not alone for long. Officer Samson had been stationed a few feet from the alley's entrance. Most men would have been ignorant of the Black Bat sneaking past them, so skilled was the Bat at not being seen. Officer Samson, however, had been raised in a small town in upstate New York. As a child, he had been taken under the wing of a grizzled old hunter, his grandfather, who had taught him how to survive in the wilderness and live off the bounty provided by the forest. Many long nights alone in the darkness of the desolate woods had added keenness to the young cop's sense of hearing that was beyond that of most men. He had heard the slight sound made by the Bat's grappling hook, and now he made his way around the corner into the alley. He looked up and could just barely see the shadowy mass of a dark-clad body scaling the vertical brick. "Stop!" shouted Samson.

The Black Bat glanced down and saw the policeman enter the alley, gun drawn. He hastened his ascent up the wall. A shot rang out. The bullet whizzed by, ripping a little hole in the black cloak which hung from his shoulders, but missing his body by inches, and hitting the wall with a sharp ping! That was one of the reasons he wore the long, flowing cloak. When a gunman could not tell where the cloak ended and the flesh began, it made it all the more difficult to aim, especially when firing upwards at a moving target.

Samson managed to get another shot off, but this one was further off target, as the young cop was somewhat flustered by having missed the first time. The Black Bat did not look down again. It was better to climb quickly, ignoring the danger below. He did listen, though. The other police had come running at the sound of the gunshots. All five of them had gathered below now. Good, thought the Bat, at least they were all in one place now. It would take time for them to get inside the building and find him once they were in. with a little luck, he could carry out his objective with no more police interference. He reached the roof and pulled himself over the edge just as the bullets of all five cops' guns flew upwards. The timing of it saved his life, for there was no way that all five could have missed while firing simultaneously had he not moved out of range at precisely that moment. He heard them all shouting below as he moved quickly to the rooftop entrance to the building.

Inside, Reinhardt and his men heard the sound of rapidly fired guns outside. It could have been anything, thought the Nazi officer, but he wouldn't take any chances. He barked orders to his men. They dropped their forks and knives and reached for their pistols. As they stood ready for anything, Colonel Reinhardt himself walked over to the closed door of the apartment's closet, knocked three times on the door, and muttered a short phrase, "Fritz! Awake and stand ready!" then turned and got into position with his men. Reinhardt and one lieutenant crouched behind the bed, while the other two each stood in one corner of the small room. All had guns drawn.

The Black Bat easily found the rooftop door that led inside the apartment building. There was no more need for subtlety, he thought to himself, as he shattered the door with a powerful kick. The thunder of the gunfire had already alerted anyone within earshot that something dramatic and violent was transpiring here tonight. He swiftly descended the narrow staircase and began to roam the halls of the building, looking for the right apartment, number 7B. He found it quickly enough. He had seen or heard no one in the halls. It was late and the people who lived there were probably asleep or, if they had been roused by the noise of the bullets, had wisely elected to remain in their rooms. He paused outside the door to 7B, took a deep breath, pulled his twin pistols from his belt, one in each hand, and kicked in the door. It gave way immediately, and as the shards of wood splintered in every direction, he took one step forward into the apartment.

His eyes darted back and forth quickly and he was instantly aware of two men, one on either side of him, with guns drawn, taking aim. Most men would have fired at them, but not the Black Bat. He did shoot, but not to take out the gunmen. He fired his two weapons in opposite directions, striking the room's two lamps. Glass shattered! Shards of jagged lamp flew and the room was plunged into nearly complete darkness. The Black Bat now had the advantage. Thanks to the miracle of his vastly improved vision, he could see perfectly, even in the near-total absence of light. Now he fired his guns again. Two short bursts! Spak-spak! The two Germans who had been ready to shoot him down were shot down themselves. They fell, and the Black Bat looked for the next danger to come. Colonel Reinhardt and his remaining lieutenant sprang up from behind the bed, but their eyes had not yet adjusted to the sudden dark, and they fired wildly, missing their intended target. The Bat shot back, hitting the Nazi lieutenant in the chest, killing him instantly. Reinhardt tried to dodge the hail of bullets. He nearly moved away unscathed, but one bullet grazed his shoulder, just enough to cause a sharp burst of pain. He fell backwards, landing seated on the floor. The pain did not prevent him from calling out, "Fritz! Now! Come now!"

At the sound of the Nazi colonel's orders, an ominous sound burst forth from the corner of the room. A great cracking! The sound of a door being ripped open, not kicked as the Bat had done to the apartment door, but literally torn in two by a pair of grotesquely huge hands. His eyes looking through the shadows with his unique night vision, the Black Bat watched in shock as the closet door burst, spewing forth an immense giant of a man, a twisted deformed monster! The 'Fritz" that Colonel Reinhardt had summoned was no mere German soldier, but some terrible freak of nature, or perhaps the result of an awful and grim scientific procedure. He, or it, as some might be tempted to call the thing, was at least seven feet tall, bulky and oak-tree like in every possible way. It had a terribly ugly face, with a hideously pug-like nose, eyes of two different sizes, a mouth that was twisted in such an odd way that it looked like it was impossible for the creature to speak, and a forest of small bunches of different lengths of hair sprouting from his scalp. Its limbs were massive and supernaturally muscled. It came skulking out of the closet like a vision from some hellish nightmare. A low gurgling noise emanated from the deformed mouth as it leaped forward to assault the Black Bat. Partially because he was a bit stunned by the sight of the thing, and partially because it moved so unexpectedly fast for its size, the Black Bat was unable to fire his guns in time, and 'Fritz' tackled him to the floor.

The two men, one a shrouded avenger of the night and one a beast from the bowels of Hades, fell together in a tangled heap of violence! The Black Bat's guns were knocked loose from his grip as they landed on the floor. He would have to fight the monster physically. Shooting the walking horror straight back to Hell was no longer an option. Fritz had his hands around the Bat's throat, while the Bat's hands were on the giant's forearms, desperately trying to keep the pressure of those gargantuan fingers from snapping his neck like a dry twig. He brought his knee up in a desperate maneuver to hit the giant German in a vulnerable area, but it seemed to have no effect, as if the beast-man were impervious to pain.

On the floor a few feet away, Reinhardt felt inside his jacket to be sure that his precious cargo, the vial containing the remaining portion of Professor Crandall's deadly serum, was still intact. It was. He watched the struggle taking place in front of him, his eyes having adjusted enough to make out the huge form of Fritz about to strangle the black-clad mystery man to death. He still had his pistol in hand, but hesitated to fire for fear of hitting his monstrous minion.

The Black Bat decided to gamble. He knew that releasing his grip on the giant's wrists would quickly allow the necessary force to strangle him, but he knew he would lose the desperate struggle soon enough anyway. Letting go with one hand, he poked Fritz in the left eye. That worked. The monstrous thing could feel pain after all! A surprisingly shrill whimper escaped from the creature's lips as it let go of the Bat's neck and reached for its eye. The pain and shock was only momentary and the huge hands quickly came down again, trying to regain their grasp on the throat of

"...the Black Bat watched in shock as the closet door burst..."

the Black Bat. The Bat, however, would not allow the giant paws to rely on the same strategy. He rolled slightly to one side, dodging the searching twisted fingers. Fritz's claws only snagged the fabric of the Black Bat's mask, ripping the cover from his face. At that moment, the room was suddenly flooded with light from the window. The police were swarming all over the area now and had reached the roof of the next building. Their flashlights were giving off enough light to brighten the apartment where the desperate struggle was taking place. The mask came off, the light came in, and Fritz saw the face of the man he was trying to murder. Having come from far abroad, the giant Nazi monstrosity did not recognize the face of Tony Quinn, but he could not ignore those jagged scars that ran down the sides of his would-be-victim's face. When one sees something completely unexpected, the result is almost always a second's worth of stunned immobility. Such was the case now, and the unmasked Black Bat took full advantage of it. Gathering every ounce of strength he had, he gave a mighty shove with both hands, sending Fritz reeling backwards. The Black Bat was free to move again! He rolled over on the floor, managing to grab his guns from where they had landed. Then he stood. From the corner of his eye, he could see Colonel Reinhardt bolting out the door. He wanted to chase him, but now the towering form of Fritz had gotten to its feet. With no hesitation, not an ounce of mercy, he unleashed a stuttering shower of bullets in the direction of the freakish behemoth. Bullets riddled the giant's chest, shoulders, face and he flew backwards, his dying bulk hitting the window and his tremendous weight crashing through the glass and the partially rotted wooden frame. Fritz, the gigantic monstrosity of the S.S. plunged to the ground below. No matter how strong the brute had been all those bullets, followed by that terrible fall, had killed him.

Perfect, thought the Bat. The falling body of that thing would distract the attentions of the police for a minute or two. He was free to pursue the one remaining German. He raced into the corridor as quickly as he could. As he ran he felt a sharp pain in his side. Crashing to the floor with the huge ape of a Nazi on top of him had cracked a rib or two. His disciplined mind put the pain aside and he continued to go after Reinhardt. He saw him at the end of the hallway and opened fire, but the German evaded the bullets by turning a corner at the last possible second. Up ahead, the Bat heard the sound of a door slamming. He forced his aching legs to run faster. Turning the corner that Reinhardt had turned a second before, he came to the door to the staircase. He fired his guns through the door once first, in case the German was waiting to ambush him. Then he pulled it open and went through. There was a slight trail of blood leading down the stairs. So, he observed, he had wounded him, but there wasn't enough blood to indicate a serious injury. He flew down several flights of stairs and out the front door. The Nazi must have made it to the street, he thought, disappointedly.

The Black Bat ran out onto the midnight streets of the city. It was rare that he would move along the streets without seeking cover, but he had no choice now. It was late, luckily, and the police activity and gunfire had made everyone who might be out opt to go indoors instead. The police were all occupied, either searching the building room by room or trying to figure out what to make of the huge, grotesque carcass that had just hit the pavement. As he ran, he put his mask back in place. He could hear the sound of frantic running footsteps up ahead of him and he knew it must be the German who had fled. Once again, the Bat forced his legs to run faster. The ache in his ribs was getting worse, but he had to persevere, had to keep moving. He had to finish this tonight.

Turning the next corner, he saw, in the distance, the shape of the running Nazi. If he could just close the gap he might be able to get to him. He needed to get closer if he was to fire his guns accurately while running. He didn't want to risk sending stray bullets flying on the streets, no matter how deserted they might look at midnight. He ran and ran, glad for the daily workouts that had toughened his muscles and given him a greater willpower. He inched a bit closer to Reinhardt, and he had an idea. Perhaps he wouldn't have to shoot on the open streets. Still running at top speed, the Bat reached down to his belt and pulled out his rope with its grappling hook. He had to time this perfectly, he thought to himself. Eyes locked on his fleeing target, arm reeled back and poised to fly forward like a striking cobra, he aimed. The rope flew forward, guided by the weight of the soaring hook on its head. The Black Bat's aim was true. The sharp hook on the end of the long rope stabbed into Reinhardt's shoulder, sinking into flesh and striking bone! The German let loose a cry of agony. The Black Bat stopped in his tracks and gave a hard yank on the end of the rope that was still in his hands. The Nazi fell backwards, landing on his back and cursing in pain. His hand shot up, holding his pistol. He was going to take one last desperate shot at the Bat! But as he pulled the trigger, the pain of his injured shoulder shot up his arm like a lightning bolt, shaking his aim and sending his bullet careening into empty air. The Black Bat's aim, however, served him well yet again. No longer moving, Reinhardt made a much safer target, and the Bat ended his life with one well placed gunshot from twenty feet away.

The Black Bat could not afford to remain in the area any longer. He had slain all the German spies, but he heard the footsteps of the approaching police and knew he had to get away quickly. Injured and exhausted, he worried that he might not be able to get away without injuring the cops if they got any closer. He knelt down by the corpse of Colonel Klaus Reinhardt, reached into the German's jacket, and retrieved the little bottle of deadly poison. He tucked the vial away in his own belt, and then pulled out something else; a tiny black symbol in the shape of a bat. He placed this on the forehead of the dead German colonel. This was his personal calling card, the sign of The Black Bat, and was a major part of giving him his fear-instilling reputation among the criminal element of the city for which he sought justice. His business here finished, the Black Bat retreated into the shadows, blending perfectly into the darkness, invisibly leaving behind a job mercilessly done.

Tony Quinn thought about the irony of the art of disguise as he prepared for the grim and vengeful task that lay ahead of him. For once he would dish out his brutal brand of justice not as the Black Bat, but as a less conspicuous sort of man.

More than a month had passed since The Black Bat had killed Klaus Reinhardt and his henchmen. His broken ribs had healed and he felt fine. After the immediate Nazi threat to the people of New York had been resolved, he had taken a short time to recover from the ordeal and regain his strength. The coroner's office had never really decided what had caused the mysterious deaths of Captain Henderson, Herman Edwards, and Sister Mary Eugenia. It didn't matter too much to the public. People tended to have short attention spans, and when the press moved on to new stories, so did they. No real effort was made to blame the poisonings on the Black Bat. Lieutenant McGrath, Quinn had heard through his sources at the city attorney's office, was disappointed at the police department's failure, once again, to apprehend the Black Bat, but was still too honorable of a detective to try to connect the vigilante to the killings with no hard evidence.

Now business in Manhattan had returned to normal. Quinn was busy with several court cases. He spent his days at the office, his evenings with Carol Baldwin as often as possible, and his late nights on patrol as the Black Bat. He had done a little research while waiting for his ribs to heal.

He had located a certain man that he had been looking for, and it was now time to pay a debt.

The irony that he had been thinking of was the fact that he, a man who the general public thought of as being blind, was about to embark on a mission for which he would assume the guise of a sighted man. The truth was, of course, that except for a brief period of several months in darkness, he had been able to see all along. It was the blindness that was a cover.

Quinn stood in front of the mirror and carefully and precisely donned his disguise. He took off his dark glasses and put them aside. He brushed his hair back, applied some grease to keep it slicked back, and applied some powder to make it appear lighter than usual. To his face he applied some theatrical makeup, blending it perfectly with the skin on both sides of his eyes to conceal the distinctive claw-mark type scars that decorated it. He dressed himself in a suit that was cheaper, and of a lighter color than those he usually wore. He had altered his physical looks, but even more importantly, he would be going out openly as a man who could see. There would be no dark glasses, no white cane, and no motions of feeling for things with his hands. This change in movement and habit would be the most important part of his disguise. It was highly unlikely that if he ran into anyone he knew they would realize that this sighted, light haired young man was the same person as the blind, scarred attorney that they were used to seeing.

Attired as someone other than himself, Tony Quinn rented a car and drove himself out of Manhattan and into the neighboring state of New Jersey. He traveled south until he reached one of the state's universities. He parked and got out of the car, then took a few moments to enjoy his thoughts. It was the first time in several years that he had had the chance to go out on a warm and sunny day without having to view the world through the dark lenses of a blind man's glasses. The grass looked bright and green, the air smelled clean and sweet, and he was even able to turn his head at the young college girls who walked past him as he stood and admired the day's beauty.

After a few minutes had passed, he let his thoughts return to the perilous adventure of the previous month and the horrors inflicted on the people of New York. That was the reason he had come to the college on this day. It was here that he had come to tie up the one loose end of that whole dark affair.

He reached into his car and took out a stack of thick books. He felt the inside of his jacket pocket to make sure he had a certain necessary item with him. Then the disguised young attorney and moonlighting avenger of injustice began his walk across the campus. With his light-colored suit and slicked back hair, the people he passed would assume he was just another young college professor on his way to class. He made his way to the building that housed the sciences department. Once inside, he headed to the biology wing. He walked down the hallway until he had reached a certain office. The door was open and Tony Quinn peered inside. Behind the desk sat a middle-aged man with a brown moustache and bushy gray hair. He was busily grading some papers and taking an occasional sip from a mug of steaming hot tea that rested atop a folded napkin.

Quinn gently tapped on the open door. The gray haired man looked up. "Can I help you, young man?" he asked.

Tony Quinn smiled. He intentionally made himself appear a little nervous. "Professor Crandall? I'm sorry to bother you, Sir. My name is Jack Meadows. I'm just starting here at the university, over in the law department. Science is kind of a hobby of mine, Sir, and I was wondering if you wouldn't mind signing my copy of your book. I really enjoyed reading it, Professor. I found it fascinating."

The professor smiled and responded, "Of course I wouldn't mind, Mister Meadows. I'm always happy to hear that people enjoy my books. I hope you found it educational as well as entertaining."

Crandall took the book from Quinn's hands and bent over it to sign it on the title page. As he was signing and deriving obvious pleasure from being asked to autograph it, he was too distracted to notice Tony Quinn's hand taking a tiny glass vial from his jacket pocket and stealthily pouring its contents into the mug of tea.

Quinn took the book back, thanked the professor, and left the office. He went back to his car, drove back to Manhattan, doffed his disguise, and went back to his legal work.

Professor Crandall's lifeless body was discovered later that afternoon. Blood had seeped into the carpeted floor of his office and soaked most of the papers on his desk. The last of the liquid death he had created had been consumed by its creator. The circle had been completed.

The End

"Faces in the New York Night"

To be honest, I had never heard of The Black Bat until a few days before I started to write "Unholy Terror." I had heard that Airship 27 Productions was looking for writers for their line of pulp stories, so I sent an inquiry to Ron Fortier. He wrote back and asked for a sample of my writing. I sent one, he liked it, and he sent me a list of characters to choose from for my first project for the pulps. I quickly went to the internet and looked for information on these old, somewhat obscure characters. When I learned a little about The Black Bat, I knew this was the one with which to begin. Why? Because even with no previous familiarity, I felt like I knew this guy!

The Black Bat might have been unknown to me, but I knew his "brothers." There is a specific genealogy when it comes to costumed vigilantes and crusaders. It's a certain class of archetype that arises when one thinks of masks and dimly lit alleys and nocturnal fights to the death. All these great characters, whether being born in the pulps or the comics, have things in common. At a glance, I could see that The Black Bat was a close relative of Batman (that's the most obvious one), Daredevil (a blind attorney and masked hero, as opposed to an attorney who pretends to be blind and is also a masked hero), and The Shadow, who has the deadly and merciless gun-wielding ferocity that is missing from the later comics-based heroes.

I was immediately comfortable thinking in terms of possible scenarios in which to place The Black Bat and his alter ego, Tony Quinn. I worked out a rough idea for a plot, and then I got to work. The opening scene included something I had been dying to use for weeks. I had awoken one morning with a vague fragment of a dream in my mind. It was the sort of dream that mostly dissipates with the coming of day, but leaves the slightest trace behind. I have no idea what the bulk of the dream had been about, but I was left with the line, "Bring the money to the man by the pinball machine." That line, of course, wound up being the orders of a crime lord to his nervous accountant. That started the ball rolling, and I had a blast writing the rest of the story.

Credit must of course by given where it is due, and I must thank the original writers of The Black Bat's pulp adventures for creating the fascinating dual identity of the once-blind man who can now see better than anyone else, but who still wears the disguise of blindness to conceal his nighttime crusades.

I must also mention the great little supporting cast that comes with Tony Quinn. We have the gorgeous Carol Baldwin, benefactor and friend (and maybe more) to the courageous young lawyer. There is also Silk Kirby and Butch O'Leary, the Bat's pair of assistants. Like many great fictional duos, these guys are opposites who complement each other; one small and sly, one big and bombastic and brutal. Then we have the two cops. Commissioner Jerome Warner looks like a high-ranking police official is supposed to look. He has the tall, square-jawed look of a John Wayne or a Clint Eastwood. He projects the image of a tough heroic cop, but under the surface, he's probably the less intelligent, or at least less imaginative of the two main police characters from the original Bat stories. The other, Detective Lieutenant McGrath is the one I found to be far more interesting. I imagine him to be of the same class as Peter Falk's brilliant portrayal of Columbo. He's a bit of a slob. He smokes cheap cigars, his clothes never look ironed, and he's certainly not handsome in any usual sense of the word. In short, he's not the type who impresses anybody by his mere presence or appearance. But he's a good cop, a smart cop. In fact, he even knows, or at least has strong suspicions of, who The Black Bat really is under that mask! It's only the fact that Tony Quinn is just a fraction smarter than poor old McGrath that keeps the lieutenant from proving his case. Despite his being a royal pain in the backside, McGrath is not a bad guy. He's a good honest cop who really does try to do the right thing. I like him as a character. He was fun to write about.

One of the most enjoyable things about writing "Unholy Terror," for me, was getting a chance to create all the other characters that had to populate The Black Bat's world for this story to be told. By the time I was done with the story, I had become quite fond of the power-hungry Captain Henderson, the immaculately dressed (in the weirdest way) Willard Speck, the irreverent nun Sister Mary Eugenia, poor Officer Sweeney (so eager to help, but so squeamish at the sight of blood), the pompous Danton Cassidy, the ruthless Colonel Reinhardt (Nazis make great villains, don't they?), the massive and deformed Fritz, and Professor Crandall, whose twisted love of science had created a little Frankensteinian horror in liquid form. Alas, as must happen to so many good pulp characters, the majority of these creations wound up dead. So, I leave them buried and lost, destroyed by the merciless brand of justice that is handed out by The Black Bat.

I hope to have the opportunity to visit this particular version of late '30s Manhattan again, to write more adventures for the Bat and his cast. I'm having too much fun to stop now.

AARON SMITH - is the author of 24 published stories, many of them for Airship 27 Productions. His pulp work includes a story in the first volume of *Black Bat Mystery*, three Sherlock Holmes stories, the Dr. Watson novel *Season of Madness*, and stories featuring Ki-Gor, Dan Fowler, and his own creations, Hound-Dog Harker and the Red Veil. His novels include *Gods and Galaxies* and *100,000 Midnights*. Information about his work can be found on his blog at www.godsandgalaxies.blogspot.com

A Black Bat Adventure

by
Joshua Reynolds

There was a duet of snarls as the twin pistols sang out, splitting the calm of the night. A lean black shape raced across the rooftop, trailing spent bullet casings and a spatter of blood.

It was 1940, and the street corners and back alleys of Red Hook echoed with the news-the Black Bat had been brought to bay at last. Officers from six precincts had joined the hunt, and the sound of sirens split the night from the Hudson to the airfield. Rifle fire plucked at the brick chimneys and pigeon coops that the Black Bat wove through in his headlong flight. Searchlights sprang from the street, trying to pin their quarry in place with blazing beams.

Tony Quinn, lawyer, scholar and vigilante, cursed as one such beam swept over him, briefly making him visible to his pursuers. A Thompson machine gun spat a flurry of lead hornets that chewed the brickwork beneath the Black Bat's feet, prompting him to spread his arms and dive from his perch.

He smashed awkwardly into a fire-escape and clawed at the iron railing. The wound in his side stretched and a ripple of pain spread through him like fire. Cursing a blue-streak through gritted teeth, the Black Bat hauled himself up as a gunfire struck the fire-escape, sending out a spray of sparks.

Voices blared through bullhorns, but he ignored them, concentrating instead on the window in front of him. He struck the glass with his shoulder and half-fell into a kitchen. He rolled across a table and dropped to the floor. Twin .45's in hand, he rose to his feet and met the frightened eyes of the family whose evening dinner he'd ruined. They stared at him in open-mouthed shock, pasta dripping from their forks.

"Sorry. Bit pressed for time," the Black Bat said, heading for the front door of the apartment. Without stopping, he kicked it off its hinges and barreled into the hall beyond. From there, he crossed the hall and hit the opposite door, barging into that apartment, pistols held low as he aimed himself like a human arrow at the window he knew would be ahead of him somewhere. A man came out of the bathroom, a toothbrush stuck in his mouth, as the Black Bat charged past.

The Black Bat ignored him as he raised his pistols and fired at the window before him, blowing the glass out of the frame in a shower of glittering shards. The way clear, he twisted his body into a swimmer's dive and leapt through the window. The membranous cape that extended from his gloves to his armpits flared, catching an updraft, and his fall slowed, but not by much. Twisting, he angled himself and crashed onto the top of a police car as it skidded up to the sidewalk. Scrabbling at the roof as his muscles howled in protest, the Black Bat rolled off of the vehicle and hit the street. Hard.

Breathing heavily, he shoved himself to his feet, pistols swinging up even as a uniformed police officer staggered out of the car. His eyes widened as he saw the Bat, and his hand dipped for his service revolver.

"Don't," the Black Bat said harshly, aiming his Colts.

The officer's hands sprang away from his belt and into the air. "Take it easy…" he said.

"Not tonight, unfortunately," the Black Bat said, backing away, blood running down his black-clad leg from the wound in his side. "Stay safe, officer." He turned and sprinted for the nearest alleyway.

A duo of police cars screeched around the corner, moving to intercept him. He skidded to a stop and spun, heading in the opposite direction. A pistol cracked and he felt a bullet pluck at his cape, but he didn't stop.

The growl of a super-charged engine blistered the air suddenly, and a battered looking coupe forced its way through the police cars, shoving them aside in a shower of sparks and the shriek of scraped metal.

The Black Bat slowed, and allowed the coupe to slide past him. A door popped open and he jumped, grabbing on and swinging himself into the back of the vehicle. The driver gunned the engine, and it sped off, outracing the police cars and disappearing into the maze of streets that made up Red Hook.

As the sound of sirens faded, the Black Bat stripped off his mask and leaned back, his lungs working like a bellows. His acid-scarred features went slack as the adrenalin left his system, and he looked down wearily at the bloody patch on his side.

"Mr. Quinn? Are you hurt?"

Quinn looked up into the puffy features of one of his aides, who was leaning over the back of the front passenger seat. Butch O'Leary was a broken-nosed reject of the squared circle and a former leg-breaker, with knuckles like jagged stone and a jaw to match. His eyes were concerned as he took in his employer's bloody state.

"Just a graze. Nothing a whiskey and a bandage won't fix," Quinn said. "Home, Silk," he continued, turning his attentions to the driver. "And quick."

"Yes sir," Silk Kirby said, his narrow features wrinkling up into an expression similar to Butch's. A former con-man and jailbird, Silk's loyalty was unquestionable. And, like Butch, he had come to care for his young employer. "Perhaps, though, a hospital might be-"

"No," Quinn snapped. "We can't take that chance. Not tonight." His scarred face grew pale. "Not tonight…"

"What happened boss?" Butch said. "The cops was all over you…more so than usual, I mean."

Quinn leaned forward, cradling his face in his hands. "I killed a man, Butch," he said, quietly.

Butch grunted in confusion. "Yeah? But ain't that what you usually do?"

"This time it was a cop," Tony Quinn said slowly. He looked up, eyes dark with suppressed emotion. "I killed a cop, Butch. I killed an innocent man."

O'Leary's jaw fell open in an expression that, at any other time, might have been comical. Silk cursed virulently, his fist pounding the top of the steering wheel. "Are you sure?" he said.

Quinn hesitated. Images flashed through his mind. A man's frightened face, fingers clawing for what he'd thought was a gun, but had been, in the end, a badge. It was the last bit that rested most heavily in his mind…a bloodstained badge, skittering across a cement floor.

"Mr. Quinn?" O'Leary said.

Quinn didn't answer, and the coupe drifted into the night silently.

By the next morning, the headlines shrieked out the answer to Silk's question. Every morning edition carried some variation on the theme.

UNDERCOVER POLICE OFFICER MURDERED BY VIGILANTE. HERO-COP GUNNED DOWN BY MASKED CRIMINAL. BLACK BAT SLAUGHTERS INNOCENTS.

Page after page of the same.

Commissioner Jerome Warner dropped a copy of the *Daily Globe* on the desk in front of him and sighed in disgust. "This is the straw, sure enough."

"Straw?" said his guest.

"That broke the camel's back. You know that old saying, Mr. Anthony?" Warner said. An older man, with steel gray hair and a bearing that bespoke military experience, Warner was dressed in a starched uniform, golden buttons and braiding contrasting with the blue.

The man sitting across from him smiled slightly and nodded. "I believe so, yes. An apt phrase if there ever was one, for a situation like this. And please, call me Jim."

Jim Anthony reclined slightly, causing the seat to creak. He was a big man, but lithe, with a simmering feline ease to his posture that bespoke a readiness to leap into action at any time. With skin burnt bronze by a lifetime under the sun, and piercing eyes, he was an imposing figure of a man. A tycoon of the best sort, he was a philanthropist and the publisher of the *Daily Star*, one of the few newspapers NOT running an attention getting headline in the wake of recent events.

Anthony was also the foremost murderist in the nation, accredited such by both amateurs and professionals alike. It was in this capacity that he had been invited to visit the police commissioner this morning, he knew. And, he knew the reasons for that invitation.

"Jim, then. You heard, I trust?" Warner said, laying his hands flat on his desk. "Hard not to I figure, not with every newsstand and street-vendor screaming about it."

"I heard. Is it true?" Jim said softly, observing Warner over the tops of his interlaced fingers.

Warner heaved a sigh. "Yes."

"Are you certain?"

"Of course I'm certain! I saw the body with my own two eyes!" Warner barked, pointing two fingers at his eyes. "It was Vincent Leonardi, as sure as I'm sitting here. Drilled clean through, with that monster's brand burned into his cheek!" He leaned back, eyes closed. "We should have stopped him sooner," he said.

"Implying that you had the opportunity," Jim said. "Is that the case?"

"You asking as a detective, or as the publisher of a newspaper?" Warner asked.

Jim chuckled. "Strictly the former. That is why you asked me here, isn't it?"

"I need him caught. Preferably yesterday." Warner scratched his chin, his eyes contemplative. "And I think you're the only one who can do it."

"What about the government? The FBI might have some interest," Jim said.

"I talked to some hard-voiced sonnuvagun…Fowler, I think his name was. He said I should call you."

"Hmph." Jim sat back. He'd worked with Dan Fowler before, and a recommendation was as good as praise from Caesar where the taciturn G-man was concerned. "So I was your second choice, huh?"

"You did a lot of good work for my predecessor, Jim. But, times change," Warner said, face flushing. "The New York City Police Department can't rely on outside agencies to clear cases. We have to stand on our own two feet-”

“Peace, Commissioner,” Jim interrupted. “I meant nothing by it.”

Warner blew out a breath and sat back. “I'm sorry. I'm just-ah.” He shook his head wearily. “I haven't slept. This whole thing…”

“I understand,” Jim said. “I've made an idle study of our resident vigilante in the months since his first appearance. Purely for speculative purposes, of course,” Jim said, gesturing idly. “Like any predator, he has definite patterns to his behavior. It should be simple enough to corner him-”

It was Warner's turn to interrupt. “Ha! I'll believe that when I see it. To give the devil his due, he's a slippery one. It's like he's got eyes everywhere-ah! Tony!” Warner surged to his feet, a smile spreading across his face.

A young man was shown into Warner's office by his secretary, and the Commissioner fairly leapt to take his hand. Jim stood, his eyes drifting first to the scars that rose from behind the young man's dark glasses, then down to his white cane.

“Jim, I want to introduce you to Tony Quinn, one of our best and brightest. Tony, this is Jim Anthony-”

“Publisher of the *Daily Star* and a philanthropist of note,” Quinn said quietly, extending his hand. Jim took it, one eyebrow going up as he felt the subtle strength in the other man's hand. “Also something of a consulting detective.”

“Not as much these days. I have my hands full with other responsibilities,” Jim said. “In Europe, mainly. I have to say, I was singularly impressed by your tenure as District Attorney. The way you handled the Maroni case was pure poetry.”

Quinn smiled crookedly. “I had quite a bit of help from the Police Department.”

“Tony is in business for himself these days, private practice, you know, but he still does a bit of consulting for his old friends,” Warner said, patting Quinn paternally on the shoulder. “Tony, Jim's here about our bat problem.”

“Bat problem?” Quinn seemed taken aback. “The Black Bat?”

“None other,” Jim said. “I understand that you've had a run-in or two with the man in question yourself.”

“Now, now,” Warner said. “I'm sure Tony didn't come here for a third-degree.”

Jim subsided, smiling good naturedly. Quinn coughed and his off-center gaze came to rest near Warner. “I heard about Officer Leonardi,

Commissioner. I wanted to know if there was anything I could do to help."

"No lad, no. Not yet at any rate," Warner said, returning to his desk. "I may call on your services later, however, when we finally bring that madman in."

"Mr. Anthony is so confident then?" Quinn said, cocking his head.

"Mildly certain, rather," Jim said. "I have a few thoughts and theories that might suffice to bring our man to bay. Of course, all of that is dependent on the answers I get to a few questions."

"For me?" Warner asked.

Jim nodded. "For anyone who might know why Officer Leonardi was where he was last night. Why he wound up in our friendly neighborhood vigilante's gunsights."

"To be honest, I'm curious about that as well," Quinn said. "The Black Bat has never gone after members of the law enforcement community before."

Warner sat back, fingers drumming on his desk. "I'm not sure that's pertinent."

"A famous member of my fraternity once said that pertinence is purely a matter of perspective," Jim said, sitting back down. "I can't determine what's useful until I know everything, pertinent or not. And the first thing I need to know about is the victim."

"Hmp." Warner eyed Jim. Then, he leaned forward. "It was an undercover operation. Very hush-hush. Tony, Mr. Anthony has the necessary clearance, but you…"

"Not for my ears, eh?" Quinn said, smiling crookedly. "I understand. I'll step out and let you two get down to it." He made his way effortlessly to the door and Warner sprang to open it for him. The Commissioner closed the door and turned.

"Smart lad. But I can't take the chance he'd say the wrong thing to the wrong person. Too many social functions, too many friends."

"And I don't, is that it?" Jim said, chuckling.

Warner coughed. "No. But you've been involved with police work for over a decade. You know the game in a way Tony, bless him, doesn't." Warned clenched his hands into fists. "You probably know we've had some problems since the repeal of Prohibition. A lot of dark corners came to light. A lot of bad apples bobbed to the surface of the barrel."

Jim waved a hand. "You have a way with metaphors," he said. "But plain facts always serve best, I've found."

Warner's face moved through several interesting shades as he struggled to say what was on his mind. Finally, he made a strangled sound and thumped the top of his desk with one fist. "I've never shied away from calling a spade a spade, Jim. Bad cops. Oh, not so many as Chicago or St. Louis, but we had-have-a bushel. Some will straighten out the further we get from the 28th Amendment, but the rest…"

"Officer Leonardi was investigating your own people?" Jim said. "Then how did he come to be at that warehouse on the Hudson last night? How did he become involved in that shoot-out with the Black Bat? And, more importantly, how did he wind up dead?"

"I think we know that last one," Warner said bitterly. "The Bat killed him, as pitilessly and remorselessly as a man might squash a bug."

Outside Warner's office, Quinn jerked back from the door. The venom in his old friend's voice was a palpable thing. Memories of the night before surged up, threatening to overwhelm him.

He saw the badge again, sliding across the floor of the warehouse, striking sparks from the concrete. He saw the cop's face, lit up by the light of the automatic, and smelled the spatter of his blood. Quinn blinked repeatedly, trying to banish the memories.

The sound of footsteps caught at the edges of his superhumanly keen hearing and he cast a wary glance towards the secretary's desk. He'd asked her to arrange a ride back to his office for him, and he'd gauged that it would take her at least five minutes to do so. He caught a whiff of a familiar cologne and fought the smile that threatened to appear on his face.

"Well, well, well, what have we here?" a familiar voice said. "Adding eavesdropping to your repertoire, Quinn?"

"Lieutenant McGrath," Quinn said, turning slightly. "I heard your shoes squeaking on the carpet. I know a good cobbler, if you're interested."

McGrath was a big-boned man, dressed in rumpled clothing and with a face like six miles of rough road. He frowned and shifted his ever-present cigar from one side of his mouth to the other. "I ain't. Why are you lurking outside the Commissioner's office, shyster?"

"Just paying Warner a visit, Lieutenant. You're obviously here on police business, however. Something to do with the Leonardi case?"

"Yeah, as a matter of fact," McGrath said, his eyes narrowing to slits. "Why?"

"No reason. I came to pay my respects…"

"Hell you say," McGrath snarled, interrupting. He jabbed a finger into Quinn's sternum and Tony squashed his instinctive impulse to bend the offending digit past the breaking point. "You ain't got no respect, Quinn. I know that for a fact!"

"Ease off, McGrath!" someone else barked. The big man spun, face contorting.

"You stay out of this Healy! This is between me and the shyster!"

Lieutenant Turkish Healy strode up, planting himself nose-to-nose with McGrath. Healy was lean and sallow, though no less rumpled than McGrath. He'd been on the force longer, Quinn knew, and hadn't enjoyed McGrath's meteoric rise to lieutenancy.

"Oh? I got the impression you were chatting about the Leonardi case. Which, if you'll recall, belongs to my squad as well as yours, McGrath. Cop gets drilled, we all get our hands dirty until the murder is put down. Right?" Healy said.

"Bull puckey! Vince was one of mine, Healy," McGrath's voice dropped into a low growl. "This is my case. Nobody else's!"

"If you gentlemen will excuse me," Quinn said hurriedly, extricating himself from the argument. Neither officer paid him much mind, for which he was grateful. He set off as fast as a seemingly blind man could go, making sure to swat the walls every so often. It was difficult sometimes, to remember the act, but it was necessary.

He moved down the hall at a trot, abruptly veering away from the exit and back towards the squad-room. He knew where McGrath's office was, and too, knew how untidy the man was. The likelihood that he had left some pertinent bit of information out in the open was too good an opportunity to pass up.

Quinn caught the sound of a tell-tale tread halfway through his circuit of the squad-room. He moved through the crowd of uniformed officers and detectives, responding to greetings and shaking hands. Footsteps were like fingerprints to a man with enhanced senses. The weight a man put on his foot was distinctive, and the tread that was trailing his was unfamiliar. He navigated the crowded common room, and his pursuer followed. He caught a whiff of something, incense? His eyes narrowed behind his dark glasses.

It wasn't McGrath, that much he was sure of. The urge to stop and look was almost overpowering, but he resisted. Instead, he bypassed McGrath's office and headed for the toilets, which were one floor down.

He took the stairs slowly, listening for the sound of feet on the stairs. Whoever it was made barely a scrape of sound, and seemed in no hurry to catch him. He left the stairwell, and headed for the restroom.

Quinn made a show of tapping the door and then pushed in, closing it behind him. By his calculations, he had less than four minutes. An eternity to the Black Bat.

He crossed to the window, which was set high in the wall. If memory served, the window to McGrath's office was directly above this one. With a snap of his wrist, he folded up his cane and stowed it in his coat. Then he leapt lightly to the window sill, squeezed out onto the ledge and shimmied up the wall, digging his fingers into the spaces between bricks. He was high enough up that he wasn't worried about being spotted. The window was alley-side, and people didn't look up as often as they should.

Quinn reached McGrath's window a few moments later, and cursed softly as he realized that it was locked. Fumbling in his coat, he stripped the seam from a hidden pocket hidden behind the lapel, and pulled out a flat lockout tool devised for him by Silk. He slid it between the panes of the window and used it to flip the latches. Then, grunting, he slid the window up and stepped inside.

Whatever else you could say about McGrath, he wasn't a desk jockey. It was unlikely he would be back anytime soon. Even so, Quinn knew he had to act fast. He scanned the overloaded desk and the piles of papers on the floor and on the chairs. Words leapt out at him, and bent for a closer look.

What he read hit him like a sledgehammer. He read further, feeling the pressure build in his head. He hadn't felt so ill since he'd first realized he might never see again.

His nostrils flared as he caught a whiff of incense. He looked up, eyes narrowing. A shadow passed under the door, and the handle rattled softly. McGrath had locked it, lucky for Quinn. He spun and slid out the window, shutting it with his fingertips. Then, flexing slightly, he took a breath and leapt across the gap between the sill and the wall of the opposite building. The soles of his shoes, treated with a thick rubber that was designed to absorb shocks, caught the wall and he shoved off, angling his body downward. His palms caught the wall, and he winced in pain as he pushed himself back and landed in the alley.

Breathing heavily, he stood, brushed himself off and looked up. The window was open, but no one was in sight. Had someone seen him?

A moment of panic came and went. Head down, he exited to alleyway, pulling out his cane as he joined the flow of the crowd. As he moved, he again caught a whiff of that odd scent. He risked a look, and caught sight of a broad shape moving in the opposite direction.

"Huh," Quinn murmured. Then he set his feet for home.

That night, as he donned his costume, he elaborated on what he'd learned for Silk and Butch. "According to the papers McGrath so helpfully left out-"

Butch sniggered. "How many times have you pulled that trick now?"

"According to the papers," Quinn went on, ignoring his aide. "Leonardi was investigating a leak in the department. In the past three months, half-a-dozen raids on holdings linked to the Schultz organization have come up with egg on their faces."

Silk whistled softly. "Gentleman Jack. There's a name to conjure with."

Gentleman Jack Schultz was a bogeyman of the first order for the New York area. Nastier than Capone, smarter than Rothstein, and crazier than the Dutchman by all accounts, Schultz had carved a bloody swath out of the ruins left by the repeal of Prohibition, muscling his way into territories once held by bootleggers and blind tiger-riders. Add in the occasional minor war with the Italians, the Irish and the Golden Chrysanthemum, and you had a boss who looked to make himself the boss of bosses.

The frightening thing was Gentleman Jack wasn't that far from realizing his dream.

In the end, that was why the Black Bat had made an appearance the previous night at a certain warehouse. A tip-off had led him to believe that Schultz himself would be there, meeting with someone important. Like say, a crooked cop on his payroll.

Quinn frowned, remembering his surprise when the gangsters had opened up on him with Thompsons. The battle had raged from one side of the warehouse to the other, finally culminating with Leonardi's death.

"Leonardi thought that Schultz still had a hold on someone in the department," he said, strapping on his custom shoulder holsters.

"So why was he in that warehouse meeting with Schultz's men last night?" Silk said.

"My question exactly." Quinn checked the clip of one of his Colts. "And, if I'm lucky, I'll get the answer tonight."

"The cops are gonna be out full force, boss," Butch said, rubbing his jaw nervously. "Looking for you, I mean. Heck, McGrath will probably have the dang National Guard out riding tanks through the streets!"

"I don't think it's come to that quite yet," Quinn said, smiling slightly. "However, keep your eyes peeled. Warner put a new dog on our scent… Jim Anthony."

"Holy…" Butch barked, strangling a curse before it could escape.

"I thought he retired," Silk said speculatively.

"So did I. Looks like he still keeps a hand in, however," Quinn said.

"He leapt lightly to the window sill…"

"Dig into him, Silk. I want to know everything about him. Just in case."

"Don't go toe-to-toe with him, Mr. Quinn," Butch said firmly. "If he gets his hands on you, that's it."

"That the voice of experience, Butch?" Silk said, looking at the other man with an amused expression.

"Make fun all you want, but he's a monster," Butch said, rubbing his throat as if in memory. "I was running muscle for one of the Maroni Boys back before I got my halo, and Anthony put a hurting on 'em. On me too."

Quinn looked at the big man. O'Leary was a veritable mountain of muscle, with rhino-hide for skin and steel for bones. It was nearly impossible to conceive of him being hurt. "How?" he said, curious.

"With his hands," Butch said, staring at his own. He blinked. "He likes to use them. But he's got guns too. Knives. And watch out for that belt of his." He rubbed his throat again.

Quinn and Silk shared a look. Then, Quinn pulled his cowl over his head and Tony Quinn, attorney, vanished into the shadow of the Black Bat once more.

An hour later, he was skimming across the rooftops, brick and gravel crunching beneath his feet, and questions humming through his mind.

He leapt over the gap between buildings, landing in a crouch. The police response to the warehouse raid had been too quick, he knew. Which meant that in all likelihood, they hadn't been there for him.

Had he interrupted a raid in progress? Had that been why Leonardi was there?

Or had he been there to warn Schultz?

It wasn't a pretty thought, and the Black Bat hesitated to think it, wondering whether it was the guilt talking. He'd killed cops before, but they'd been rotten to the core, and murderers to boot, which automatically rendered their status null and void as far as he was concerned.

He skidded to a stop, head cocked, listening. His fingers brushed over the clasps on his holsters, but he didn't draw the automatics.

Several of Schultz's men had escaped from the warehouse last night. One or two had bail this morning. And thanks to weeks of investigation and rooftop lurking, the Black Bat knew exactly where they'd be.

He started off again, vaulting across another gap and scrambling up onto a higher ledge. He crouched there, catching his breath. The Bronx spread out around him. It wasn't on his usual patrol route, but the men who'd escaped him the night before would be meeting at a burnt out old blind tiger. The former speakeasy hid within an Old Dutch court, off a crooked side-street. It was a bad area, with a black history to it.

The speakeasy called the Comet Club, had been owned by a man named Suydam before a fire had swept through it one night in 1921, taking the lives of several patrons, working girls and Suydam himself.

Now it was a sore spot on the topography of the city, a black tooth of brick and charred wood. In '25, someone had taken to using the gutted central area for a makeshift coliseum for bare-knuckle fights. By 1937, Gentleman Jack had begun using it to store and sell illegal goods. Or so Silk Kirby had said.

The Black Bat himself had never visited the place. It didn't do to take away all of the rats' holes, not if you couldn't be sure of exterminating them all. Instead, he let Kirby and O'Leary patrol it for him, and keep him informed about what went on in there. It was a regular font of information at times.

He didn't have time for the slow dance now, however. It would have to be fast and dirty, and if it cost him information in the future, well, that was a price he had to be willing to pay.

The Black Bat slid down the incline of one roof, and sprang to the next, dropping lightly through the gaping holes in the surface to land on a latticework of support beams. A black tarp had been stretched across the bottom of the remains of the upper level, creating a makeshift ceiling. It also effectively blocked out the lights from the goings on below. Gentleman Jack was no fool. He'd carved out a goblin market and he was wise enough to keep it out of the eyes of the unwary.

The Bat dropped onto the remains of the upper floor, ignoring the sagging doors and rotting wood. There was a faint turpentine stink in the air, and he silently cursed. Sometimes, having improved senses was less a blessing and more a curse. He could smell nothing but the twenty-year memory of the fire that had claimed this place, and the sugary stench of something else beneath it.

He reached into the harness he wore over his costume, sliding a lock-back knife out of one pocket. He snapped it open with a flick of his wrist, and drove it into the tarp, cutting out a triangle of material. Peeling back the makeshift flap, he looked down.

There were electric lights strung up all over, connected to a main military surplus generator that grumbled softly. Seven or eight tables occupied the floor, and a skuzzy-looking individual dispensed cheap drinks from behind a sagging bar. There were only five men in the house tonight, and the Black Bat recognized only two of them.

A knife-blade grin stretched across the Bat's face as he looked down at his prey. Paul Copernick and Max Garcia. Two of Gentleman Jack's more experienced muscle. They had both been at the warehouse the previous night, and had both been at the meeting with Leonardi. Which meant, like as not, they knew something.

That was the theory anyway.

Swiftly, he pulled his pistol and put a bullet into the generator. The lights flickered and died and then the Black Bat was tearing through the tarp and dropping down onto the table directly below him.

Men began yelling in panic, and a gun went off wildly. Despite the darkness, the Black Bat was able to see perfectly, and he used his advantage to the fullest. Even as he landed, and the men whose quiet game of poker he'd interrupted shot to their feet, the Black Bat jammed the knife he still held through the hand of the closest of the poker players, nailing him to the table!

As the unlucky victim screamed in pain and surprise, the Black Bat swiveled on the table, shooting out his foot to crack across the jaw of the next man. Pistol out, he fired three shots, tagging the three remaining men, though not killing them. Then he leapt from the table in silence, bounding after the bartender, who was trying to make his escape.

The Black Bat jumped from table to table, keeping pace easily with the stumbling, blind goon. With an effortless bunch of his muscles, he jumped over the hapless criminal's head and landed in front of him. The bartender ran into him and staggered back with a yelp.

The Black Bat leaned forward. "Boo," he whispered. Immediately, the acrid stink of urine filled his nose and his grin turned ugly as he clouted the man across the side of the head with his pistol, dropping him like a sack of potatoes.

"What was that? What was that?" somebody said in obvious fear. "What's going on?"

"I've been shot, that's what's going on," someone else rasped. The Black Bat turned and sauntered towards them, his rubber-soled boots making no noise on the floor.

"Oh God, I'm bleeding like a stuck pig here," the one who was nailed to the table moaned. Metal scraped wood, and the moan became a whimper.

"You'll live," the Black Bat said, his voice carrying easily.

"Who's that?" one of the others said. The Black Bat turned, watching the crook fumble about in the dark, clutching the spot where the Black Bat's bullet had creased his arm. "Who is that?"

"You know me, Garcia," the Black Bat said. He stalked towards the man. "You got away from me last night, but no man can escape me forever."

"The Bat," Garcia whispered, clambering to his feet. He reached into his coat, going for his gun. It was a desperate move for a man who was trapped in the dark, and the Bat's hand shot out, trapping Garcia's hand against his chest. Then, the Black Bat snapped out a kick into Garcia's knee, shattering it. Garcia slumped with a howl.

The Black Bat hauled him up and tossed him onto a table. He pounced on the crook, squatting over him like a demon out of hell, the barrel of his automatic pressed to the frightened man's cheek.

"In fact, two of you got away last night. Don't bother trying to run, Copernick. I see you." The Black Bat didn't bother to turn.

"What-what do you want?" Garcia hissed, trying to pull away from the cool steel of the Colt.

"Answers to persistent questions."

"What?"

"Last night. What did I interrupt, exactly?"

"I don't know," Garcia said. The Black Bat jerked him up and slammed him down.

"How about now?"

"No!"

The Black Bat thumbed back the hammer on the Colt. "And what about now?"

Garcia squeezed his eyes shut. "We was meeting a cop."

"I already know that. Why?"

"He-ah-he had some information for us! For the Gentleman!"

"For Schultz?"

"Yeah! Yeah!"

"Shut up Garcia!" someone snarled. "Don't tell that freak nothing!"

"Better yet, tell me everything Garcia," The Black Bat said, leaning close. "I want a name."

"I don't-" Garcia whimpered. The Black Bat turned slightly. "What about you Copernick? Who was the Gentleman meeting last night?"

"I ain't saying nothing, Bat." Copernick had gotten to his feet. He was a big man, built broad and square. The Black Bat had tagged him across the head, and blood flowed freely down his bulldog face. He had a revolver in his hand and was shifting back and forth, as if trying to pierce the darkness that surrounded him. "I ain't scared of you!"

"That's a pity." The Black Bat came to his feet and back-flipped off of the table. He landed in a crouch, then sprang into the air again, twisting around so that he shot past Copernick, his hands snagging the man's coat along the way.

Copernick yelled as they tumbled across the floor, his revolver skittering away. The Bat's fingers jabbed out like claws, striking nerve clusters, and the big man spasmed, going limp.

"What did you…what did you do to me?" Copernick mumbled.

"Nothing permanent, if you answer my questions," the Black Bat said, crouching over the paralyzed criminal. "Who was the Gentleman meeting? What was his name?"

"Go to hell!"

The Black Bat grabbed Copernick's hand and twisted it up. Then he took a grip on the man's fingers. "One more chance, Copernick. Then I begin taking fingers."

"You sonnuva-"

"Wrong answer," the Black Bat said. Then he broke Copernick's trigger finger, eliciting a howl. "Be awhile before you can use a gun at this rate."

Copernick's heels drummed on the floor. The Black Bat grabbed another finger. "Let's go for just holding one then."

"No! No! I'll talk," Copernick bellowed, twisting like a fish on a hook. The Black Bat sat back on his heels, but retained his hold on the man's hand and wrist.

"Who were you meeting?" he growled. "Who was he?"

"Guy… named Pisco. Danny Pisco!"

"Pisco?" the Black Bat blinked. "Not Leonardi?"

"No!"

The Black Bat stood abruptly, releasing Copernick's hand. The gunsel rolled over, limply cradling his hand. The sound of leather scraping on wood alerted the Black Bat to the approach of someone and he spun, catching a descending blow on his wrist, and popping a rabbit punch in return. Garcia folded up, dropping the switchblade he'd been holding.

The Black Bat lifted his knee, catching the crook in the chin, and sent him sprawling. Almost idly, he stepped on Garcia's throat.

A cop named Pisco. Not Leonardi. Again came the memory of the badge sliding across the floor, and the surge of wet guilt coiling in is gut like a cancer. He shook his head and looked around. "You get a pass tonight. Tell the Gentleman that the Black Bat is coming for him. Tell him that I'm going to take his organization apart."

"Tell him yourself!"

The doors flew open and shotguns snarled, chewing up tables and chairs. The Black Bat was already moving towards the newcomers, both of his automatics out and singing a reply as he slid in among them.

He caught sight of an older man with silver hair and a sneer worthy of a Roman senator before the Gentleman's bodyguards closed ranks. The Black Bat sprinted for the street, flinging lead behind him to discourage pursuit.

He hit the street as the light turned red and jumped up onto the waiting cars, crossing their hoods like a bridge to the other side of the street.

Darting into an alleyway, he swung himself up onto a fire escape and began to climb. Silk and O'Leary had orders to meet him nearby.

The light hit him like a fist as he made it to the roof, and he spun, pulling his pistols instinctively. The wound in his side burned and he bit back a groan. He fired blind, his vision compromised, and was rewarded by a sudden return of darkness and the shattering of glass.

Almost immediately, another light caught him. Then another, and another. A shape stepped between them and him, and a deep voice said, "Night vision, then?"

"What?" The Black Bat snarled, blinking.

"Your eyes…I assume you have some form of night vision enhancement to gallivant across the rooftops the way you do. Is it a mechanism, or-"

The Black Bat launched himself at the shape, swinging his pistols like clubs. The man swung agilely aside, and the Black Bat landed atop one of the lights, shattering it with his weight. Half-blind, he staggered away. He realized with a start that the roof was covered with discreet lumps of camouflaged machinery. As he moved, two more sprang on, the bright lights scraping against his enhanced eyeballs like razors.

An elbow caught him in the small of the back, and he rolled with the blow, bouncing to his feet and swinging a backhand at his opponent. His wrist was caught in a bone-crushing grip and he was snapped around like a bullwhip. A fist caught him in the belly as his shoulder was jerked painfully.

The spot where the bullet had tagged him the previous evening was screaming now, sending up flares of red lightning behind his eyes.

"That was where the bullet creased you," his opponent said, still clutching the Bat's wrist. A sharp jerk forced him to drop his pistol. "And from this position, I can dislocate your shoulder with a twist of my wrist."

The Black Bat glared up at the man. A familiar face met his gaze.

"Now, all I want to do is chat. We can do this the easy way, or the hard way. Your choice," Jim Anthony said.

"Hard. Always hard," the Black Bat said, firing his free pistol into the light closest to Anthony and sending a spray of sparks up into the other man's face. Anthony threw up a hand to protect his face, and the Black Bat wrenched his wrist free. He made the newly freed hand into a fist and drove it towards Anthony's knee.

The latter's hand flashed down, swatting the Bat's blow aside. Fingers like steel wire fastened on the back of the Black Bat's head, and he found himself jerked into the air and tossed backwards like a football. He crashed against a light, glass spattering his bodysuit, his remaining pistol flying out of his hand.

Clambering to his feet, The Black Bat's mind raced. He needed to buy himself time to recover. "Nice little ambush you set up," he growled.

"That pitch will ruin your throat, you know," Anthony said, tapping his own for emphasis. "My advice is to try a more subtle form of vocal camouflage."

"I'll keep that in mind," the Black Bat said. "This must have taken a while to set up."

"Not long, once I calculated your route," Anthony said. "I predicted that you'd hunt down the survivors of last night's little massacre. And I still have enough contacts in the underworld to lead me here. Another bit of advice? Route randomization. It'll prevent this sort of awkward encounter in the future."

"Not planning to take me in, Mr. Anthony?"

"If he's not, I sure as hell am!"

Both Anthony and the Black Bat turned. Lieutenant McGrath stepped out from behind a chimney, a Thompson clutched in both hands. Cigar smoke swirled around McGrath's bulldog face as he grinned.

"You did good, Anthony. But it's time to let the professionals do their job!" As he spoke, three more officers stepped out from behind him and spread out. Dressed in street-clothes, they hefted shotguns menacingly.

"McGrath, I told you to keep your people back-" Anthony began, raising a hand.

"And I told you that he was mine!" McGrath barked, raising the Thompson. It belted out a fiery roar, chopping through several of the lights. Anthony jumped back with a curse as the Black Bat threw himself to the side, scooping up his lost pistol as he went.

He fired, blowing out the lights closest to McGrath and his men, causing them to howl and yelp. Then he was running towards them, arms crossed over his head.

The Black Bat plowed into the cops, sending them falling like ninepins. Grabbing McGrath by his lapels, the Black Bat hauled him up and spun him around, wrapping an arm around his throat.

He pressed the barrel of his automatic to McGrath's head. "Everyone back off!"

"Now, son, you don't want to do that," Anthony said, stepping over the dazed officers, holding his hands out. "Let the Lieutenant go, and we can talk about this."

"Somebody shoot him!" McGrath snarled, clutching at the Bat's arm. "Shoot through me if you have to, but get him!"

"You know, if you nitwits had bothered to set up your ambush across the street, you could have caught the Gentleman," the Black Bat said conversationally. "That would have been quite the feather in your pointy cap, huh McGrath?"

Anthony stepped between the cops and the Black Bat, arms spread. He jerked his chin towards the street. "Only one way out of this, friend."

The Bat's eyes narrowed. What was Anthony trying to tell him? "I don't intend to turn myself in," he said. A slight smile curled at the edges of Anthony's mouth. He cut his eyes towards the street. The Black Bat's own widened in response.

He was trying to tell him something. How to escape. But why? He tensed, readying himself. It was a question for another time. Anthony's hand twitched. The Black Bat hoped that was the signal.

Anthony lunged, grabbing McGrath and spinning him around, even as the Black Bat spun and hurled himself off the roof! The night air rushed up around him and he spread his arms, letting the updraft billow up into his 'wings', slowing his descent. He twisted, controlling the angle of his fall and he landed in the middle of the street.

Adrenaline surging through him, he ignored the honking cars that skidded around him and he bent, jerking a manhole cover up and sliding it aside. Then he jumped down into the sewer, feet first.

Far above, Anthony watched as his prey disappeared below ground, and he allowed himself a small chuckle.

"What the hell are you laughing at?" McGrath snapped from behind him.

Anthony turned, his chuckle turning into an annoyed grunt. "None of your business, Mr. McGrath."

"It's Lieutenant!"

"What it is, is annoying," Anthony said crossing his arms. "Your blundering cost us the best chance we had to capture our friendly neighborhood vigilante. He'll be on his guard now."

McGrath's face went an interesting shade of red as Anthony watched. Before the apoplectic officer could reply, the squawk of a siren caught Anthony's attention. With cat-like speed he moved to the ledge and crouched, peering across the street. A moment later he straightened, smiling.

"Excellent. Well, Lieutenant Healy is on the ball at least."

He could practically hear McGrath's teeth grinding together as he swung down off the building and climbed down the fire-escape. He headed across the street to meet Healy, who was coming the other way, a shotgun over his shoulder.

"Well?" Anthony said.

"He got away," Healy said leaning forward as Anthony lit his cigarette.

"These things will kill you," Anthony said.

"Not before the stress," Healy replied. "Rounded up a few of the slower ones, if you're interested."

"But not Schultz?"

"He slipped away. If we knew where he was hiding-"

"It wouldn't matter. No, we need to catch him in the act," Anthony said, rubbing his chin speculatively. His eyes drifted towards the open manhole and narrowed. He turned back to Healy. "I'd like to chat with the ones you have in custody."

Healy grinned. "I thought you might."

Down below the street, the Black Bat paused for a minute, trying to expel the excess adrenaline that bubbled through him. Bent double, head held low, he fought to control his breathing. Then, limbs trembling, he stood, cast a last glance upwards, and then set off.

It was rare that the Black Bat was forced to use the sewers to travel, but he'd had enough foresight to long ago map out several routes. He touched the wall, seeing his mark painted on it in a phosphorescent paint that Silk had devised. There were more like it all along the way, a play on Theseus and the ball of twine.

"Let the Lieutenant go..."

Above ground, he often used a special light-reflecting tape tied around gargoyles, aerials and chimney stacks in much the same manner. It was a bit of a cheat, but often times a necessary one. Like now for instance.

It took him over an hour to locate the right sewer grate, and then a further twenty minutes to signal the men sitting inside the black car across the street. Silk pulled the coupe up alongside, but not on top of, the grate, hiding it from view and Butch leaned out, helping the Black Bat lever it loose. Pulling his employer bodily into the car, O'Leary growled, "Punch it."

"Punching," Silk said, pulling the car away from the curb and into traffic. The slim man kept his eyes out for any tails, official or otherwise, and began to circle the block."Well?" he said, after awhile.

"It's a good news, bad news situation," the Black Bat said, pulling off his mask. He stripped off his shirt a moment later, checking the bandage on his side. He touched it gingerly, wincing. "I got information, but I almost got caught." He looked at Butch. "You were right. Jim Anthony's got a hell of a punch."

O'Leary grimaced. "Damn."

"Anthony? I wondered why you were coming in via the low road," Silk said. "What happened?"

"He set an ambush is what happened." Quinn rubbed his face tiredly. "And then...then he let me go. I think."

"You ain't sure?" Butch said.

"I'm not sure of much these days." Quinn leaned back. "Pisco."

"What's a Pisco?" Silk said.

"A Pisco is who the Gentleman was supposed to meet last night. So if Leonardi wasn't there to meet with Schultz, why was he there?"

"Maybe it was an alias. You said Leonardi was looking for a mole, right? Maybe he was undercover," Silk said.

"Maybe. But none of those papers I found in McGrath's office mentioned anything about that." Quinn hunched forward. "No. I have a feeling that this Pisco, whoever he is, has the answers I need."

"And what if it turns out Leonardi was innocent, Mr. Quinn?" Silk said, quietly. "What then?"

"Then? Then I turn myself in." Quinn's tone brooked no argument.

"Boss, ya can't-" Butch sputtered.

"I have to. If I killed an innocent man..." Quinn shook his head. "No. Somebody has to pay for that."

"Maybe sooner rather than later," Silk said. "We've got a tail. A Rolls

Royce, three cars back. Plug-ugly in the driver's seat."

Quinn shifted in his seat, looking through the tinted glass of the coupe's back window. "It's Anthony."

"I remember him being handsomer than that," Butch muttered.

"I meant in the sense that it's at his direction, pal," Quinn said, slapping the big man on the arm. "Lose him, Silk."

"What do you think I've been trying to do for the past five minutes?" Silk said, jerking the wheel back and forth. The coup wove in and out of traffic, leaving behind a trail of honking horns and screeching tires. The Rolls kept pace easily, gliding through traffic like a shark.

"He's good," Quinn murmured. He turned, tapping Kirby's shoulder. "Deploy the deterrents."

"Mr. Quinn…" Silk began, hesitating.

"Do it."

"You're the boss, Boss." Silk tapped a thin lever beneath his seat. Beneath the coupe, two refurbished ammunition cans popped open, spilling a flood of specially designed caltrops into the street. Tires popped and cars skidded as the coup sped on.

Quinn looked back, and gave a grunt of satisfaction. The Rolls was caught in the tangle of cars, its tires suddenly less than effective. "That did it."

"I thought you were all for giving yourself up?" Silk said.

"After I figure out who the Gentleman was meeting, and why." Tony Quinn grinned fiercely. "I surrender on my terms or not at all."

"That's what I like to hear!" Butch said, smacking his fist into Quinn's shoulder.

Quinn smiled tiredly and sat back, his mind whirring with information. Foremost was the fact that Anthony had let him go.

As District Attorney, he'd never tried a case connected to Anthony, the man had been retired by then, for whatever value you placed on the word "retire." But he'd heard plenty about him. He wasn't a man to give up easily. Nor was he a man to let the law stand in the way of what he considered justice, something Quinn could sympathize with.

So that added up to what?

By the next morning, he still didn't have a satisfactory answer for any of the questions plaguing him. Dressed once more in civilian clothes, Quinn ascended the stairs of the precinct-house, hoping to get Warner alone. The old man was a friend, but also an open spigot at times. He could keep a secret when it counted, but rarely from his old friend Tony Quinn.

It hurt him a bit to take advantage of his friendship with Warner in such a way, but it was easy enough to rationalize away. Murder was harder to explain away, but he did that almost every day regardless.

His grip tightened on his cane and he stopped, taking a breath. Eyes closed, he let the sounds of the city play over him. There were so many faces in his mind's eye, men who'd died by his hand. They'd all deserved it, but he never stopped wondering whether or not he had the right to do as he did, or whether he was simply indulging in some mad *berserkgang*.

Then there was Leonardi. A man in the wrong place at the wrong time. He let out a shaky breath. An innocent life, insofar as he knew at the moment. Taken by his hand.

"Hey, Pisco!"

Quinn resisted the urge to snap around. That was McGrath's voice. Where?

He shifted slightly, scanning the stairs. There! A thin cop, dressed in civvies, was stopped at the foot of the stairs, looking back. Quinn recognized him as one of the men from the rooftop the night before.

McGrath stood at the top of the stairs, cigar smoke wreathing his head. "You going to Ed's?"

"It's my break, Lieutenant," Pisco said, his voice a throaty rasp. "You want something?"

"A pastrami on rye, since you asked so nicely. How's the hip?" McGrath said, concern creeping into his normally brusque tone.

Pisco slapped his hip. "Fine and dandy like sour candy, Loot. We'll get him tonight for sure."

"Take it easy anyway," McGrath said. "I want pickles too."

"Pickles," Pisco said, throwing off a lazy salute. "Got it." He turned and started down the street, limping slightly. Quinn wondered whether he was responsible for that.

"Hey!" McGrath barked suddenly. Quinn grimaced, realizing that the pugnacious policeman had seen him. "What the hell are you doing here shyster?"

"Just leaving, as a matter of fact," Quinn said, making a decision. Fate had placed Pisco in his path, and there was nothing for it but to follow him.

McGrath bounded towards him, grabbing his arm. "Healy ain't here to save your hide now, Quinn. Somebody went through my office yesterday. You wouldn't know anything about that would you?"

"How would a blind man go through your office, Lieutenant?" Quinn said. "I'm given to understand that it's hazardous enough even if you've got your sight."

"Pretty funny," McGrath said, allowing Quinn to jerk his arm free of his grip. "If it wasn't you, who was it?"

"Why don't you ask Mr. Anthony? I'm given to understand that he's a sterling detective."

"Nuts to Anthony, and nuts to you, shyster," McGrath growled. "If I find out that you're involved in this investigation, I'll…"

Quinn "accidently" jabbed his cane down on McGrath's foot. McGrath yelped and hopped back. "Do forgive me Lieutenant. Another appointment beckons. You understand." Without waiting for a reply, Quinn started down the stairs, moving in the same direction Pisco had.

Ed's was a diner one block over. It was famous for the pastrami and for the number of high-ranking city officials who graced its stools. Quinn had eaten there more than once, both on the clock and off. His presence wouldn't arouse suspicion.

He caught up with Pisco as he went in, and followed him to the counter as he gave his order. Quinn silently examined him. Pisco was tall, but built snake-lean, with a gunfighter's hands and a flat face.

Quinn ordered coffee and watched as the Detective went to the phone in the corner, made a call and sat down in one of the empty booths, just like any other customer waiting on his order.

What set him apart from the other customers was who sat down across from him five minutes later. Quinn fought to keep a hard smile off of his face as his new friend Copernick sat down and hunched towards Pisco.

They spoke in low, hushed tones, but Quinn's enhanced hearing made it seem as if they were only inches away, as opposed to across the diner.

"What happened to you?" Pisco said.

"The Bat," Copernick grunted, rubbing his splinted fingers. "He showed up at the Comet."

"Bad luck for you boys," Pisco said.

"Bad luck for you too," Copernick said.

"Oh?"

"Someone spilled your name," Copernick said, blithely side-stepping the fact that it had been him.

Pisco's face took on the consistency of lard. "And?" he said, after a moment.

"And the Bat knows you were there last night."

"Besides that," Pisco said, fingers tapping on the table. "Does he know about my-ah-relationship with the Gentleman?"

"Who can say. The Gentleman wants to talk, though."

"Good for him."

Copernick shifted uncomfortably. "He wants to talk tonight. Wants to know what you're going to do about this?"

"Keep your voice down," Pisco said. "McGrath has Leonardi's papers. Or he did. And he's got a mad-on for the Bat. The Gentleman is in the clear."

"So you say. But considering that you're the one who…"

Quinn's ears perked up at that. Pisco leaned forward suddenly, teeth bared. "Shut it, Copernick."

"Fine. I'm just here to let you know that the Gentleman wants a meet. And he doesn't want the Bat showing up like he did before, understand?"

Pisco glared at him. "Where is he going to be?"

"The penthouse. You know it?"

"I'm on the racketeering task force, what do you think?" Pisco said, standing.

"I ain't paid to think. Be there at eight, Pisco. Or maybe the Gentleman finds a new snitch, and you start learning to breathe under water."

Pisco went to the counter as Copernick left. Quinn decided to take advantage of the opening.

"Detective Pisco?" he said. Pisco looked at him warily, his eyes narrowing as he caught sight of the cane and the dark glasses.

"Who wants to know?"

"Quinn. Tony Quinn. Pleased to make your acquaintance," Quinn said, holding out his hand. Pisco looked down at the hand, then back up.

"You're Warner's pal, aren't you? Used to be DA?"

"Guilty as charged."

Pisco grunted. "How about that? A celebrity. What do you want, Mr. Celebrity?"

"Just to chat."

"About?"

"Vincent Leonardi," Quinn said, pitching his voice low.

Pisco hesitated. "What about him?"

"A source told me that you were involved with his investigation."

"What source?"

Quinn smiled. "So you were, then?"

"No," Pisco said. "Didn't even know the guy."

"But you're part of McGrath's unit, right?" Quinn pressed. "The racketeering task force?"

"So?"

"So was Leonardi. Is the task force that big?"

Pisco's eyes became slits. "Why are so interested, Mr. Celebrity?"

"A sense of civic responsibility, Detective," Quinn said. "A police officer was murdered in the course of his duty. I merely want to help."

"I think we've got it handled, thanks," Pisco said bluntly. The waitress deposited his bag on the counter and he scooped it up and stood. "I got to get the Loot his lunch. He gets cranky when he's hungry."

"The source said you were with Leonardi the night in question," Quinn said. Pisco spun, grabbing a handful of Quinn's coat, and slammed him back against the counter. Quinn rolled with the blow, forcing himself not to react.

"Whoever said that is a damn liar," Pisco hissed. "Tell me who he was, maybe I won't run you in for interfering in an investigation."

"While I'm sure your Lieutenant would love nothing better, do you really think that's wise?" Quinn said softly. "The Commissioner might be unhappy..."

Pisco's face twisted with displeasure, but he released Quinn and stepped back.

"Stay out of my way, Mr. Celebrity. Or I'll run you in, friend of the Commissioner or not."

Quinn watched him go, idly straightening his tie. Pisco was a rat, no two ways about it. And one long overdue for extermination.

The smell hit him then, that same odor of incense. He cocked his head. A finger tapped him on the shoulder.

"Fancy seeing you here, Mr. Quinn. I've been trying to get in contact with you for what seems like several days now."

Quinn turned, startled despite himself. Jim Anthony smiled at him and gestured towards a booth. "Do you have a minute?"

"I'm sorry, Mr. Anthony, but I was just on my way..."

"It won't take long." Anthony put an arm around him and maneuvered him towards the booth. Quinn winced as Anthony put pressure on the shoulder he'd nearly dislocated the night before. "How's the arm by the way?"

"What?" Quinn said.

"The arm? The way you were twisting around, I thought I was going to have to twist it out of the socket." Anthony smiled and sat back.

"I don't know what you're talking about."

"Are you actually blind, or are you pulling an act? If it's the latter, it's very impressive. Even more so if it's the former."

"Mr. Anthony…" Quinn began.

"Call me Jim. Please."

"Jim then. I honestly don't know what you're talking about. Now, if you'll excuse me," Quinn said, making to stand.

"I wish you wouldn't. We have quite a bit to talk about, you and I." Anthony knocked on the table with his knuckles. "Especially considering that you didn't actually kill Detective Leonardi."

Quinn froze, half out of his seat.

Anthony nodded. "You softened those gentlemen up quite a bit last night. Very helpful."

"You talked to them?"

"One or two. Healy made the bust while McGrath was playing with us on the roof. He arrested several of the Gentleman's men, those unlucky enough to be left behind." He reached into his coat and pulled something out. "Here's your knife, by the by. Wouldn't do to have that sitting in an evidence locker somewhere, now would it?" Anthony tossed the clasp-knife onto the table. Quinn snatched it, forgetting for the moment that he was supposed to be blind.

"Why? Quinn said.

"Why what? The knife?"

"Why everything?"

"You didn't kill Leonardi." Anthony plunked a bullet casing down on the table between them. He held it in place with his finger, and kept his eyes on Quinn. "I tested the bullet, compared it to others recovered from the scene. You use an automatic. The killer used a revolver."

"A service revolver," Quinn said quietly.

Anthony nodded. "McGrath didn't want to hear it, of course."

Quinn smiled crookedly. He wanted to slump in relief, but instead simply sat back down and laid his hands flat on the table. "McGrath would arrest me even if I took a bullet for the President."

"He is quite single-minded," Anthony, rested his chin in his palm and rolled the bullet around. "He has quite a file on you, by the by."

"Full of hearsay and rumor, no doubt."

"Surprisingly, no." Anthony looked at him. "He suspects who you are."

"Speaking of which," Quinn said.

"I am a detective, Mr. Quinn." Anthony plucked the bullet up and bounced it on his palm. "You rely too much on the camouflage your blindness and reputation provides. I had no preconceptions about you, and it only took me a day or so to put it together."

Quinn sat back, slightly affronted. "I wasn't aware that this was a peer-review."

Anthony smiled. "Relax, Mr. Quinn. I know better than anyone how much luck goes into a shadow-career like this. And I'm not planning on telling anyone."

"Why?"

Anthony looked at him silently for a moment. "Why not?" He shrugged. "It doesn't serve anyone's best interests, and, in all likelihood, those who need to know, already do."

Quinn felt a chill run down his spine. "Like who?"

Anthony's smile grew. "You've made quite a name for yourself, Mr. Quinn. Both in costume and out. Any number of organizations and individuals have been keeping an eye on you."

"You're not going to tell me?" Quinn demanded.

"I have a feeling that if I did, you'd only get yourself in trouble." Anthony stood. "My Rolls is waiting outside. Would you care for a ride?"

Bemused, Quinn stood and followed Anthony out onto the street, where the silver Rolls Royce from the night before was waiting, its tires newly replaced.

As he slid into the back, Anthony beside him, the driver turned around. Pug-faced, he frowned. "This the guy?"

"This is the guy," Anthony said, closing the door. "Tony Quinn, Tom Gentry."

"Neat trick with the caltrops," the driver said, baring his teeth. "Real neat."

"Cut him some slack, Tom," Anthony said, smiling. "Take us to where we spotted his associates earlier."

Quinn looked at him. "You spotted them?"

"Hard not to," the driver snorted.

"Is there any way I can convince you to lay low for the next few days?"

Anthony said, looking at Quinn. "Let me follow up on Detective Pisco."

"Were you there for him as well?" Quinn said, nodding to the diner. "Those men Healy arrested, they gave him up?"

"After a few hours on intense questioning," Anthony said. "And a bit of light hypnosis."

"Of course," Quinn said, good humoredly.

"Regardless, Pisco has been under suspicion for awhile, according to Leonardi's notes." Anthony looked at Quinn. "I mean, in the notes you didn't get a chance to swipe."

Quinn snorted. "I do what I have to."

"That sounds familiar," Tom muttered loudly.

Anthony pretended not to hear his driver. "As near as I can determine, Leonardi followed Pisco to that warehouse. When you showed up ..."

"Pisco killed Leonardi," Quinn said slowly.

"Most likely. Pisco has probably been on the Gentleman's payroll for several years. Since he was in uniform, even. With Warner's crackdown on corruption, he's sweating bullets. Or he should be, if he's smart." Anthony sat back. "What I can't figure out, is why he's risking going to see the Gentleman again."

"From what I've heard of Schultz, he's not the type you refuse," Quinn said, leaning his cane against his chin. A sudden thought hit him. "Wait."

"What?"

"Pisco is part of the anti-racketeering squad. Leonardi might have suspected him, but nobody else does, that's obvious. And with Leonardi dead, and me taking the blame, nobody can link him to the Gentleman except ..."

"Except the Gentleman himself," Anthony said. He clapped Quinn on the shoulder. "Smart."

"I'm something of a detective myself, you'll recall," Quinn said. "Pisco is meeting the Gentleman tonight, at someplace called the penthouse. I intend to be there, to take them both."

"Into custody?"

"Sure," Quinn said, not looking at Anthony.

Anthony frowned. "So you intend to go out again tonight?"

"I have to," Quinn said.

"Not really. Once we know where the meeting is taking place, we can simply arrest them all. I can match the bullet that killed Leonardi to Pisco's weapon, evidence enough even for the salubrious Lieutenant McGrath. With the testimonies of the men who were arrested last night ..."

"I am a detective, Mr. Quinn."

"No," Quinn said, gripping his cane in both hands. "I have to do this."

"I can't allow you to, I'm afraid," Anthony said softly, reaching for Quinn. "Your interference could destroy the case and unravel ..."

Quinn's cane stabbed out, catching Anthony in the throat. The big man gagged and crashed back against his door, grabbing for the cane. Quinn lashed out with his foot, smashing the door open. Anthony toppled backwards and Quinn went with him, sliding over the other man and throwing himself out of the Rolls.

He hit the street and rolled, scraping his hands and face. The Rolls screeched to a halt up the block, but Quinn was already up and moving. He sped into an alleyway and leaped for the bottom of a fire-escape. Quinn swung himself up and then began to climb.

Anthony was after him a moment later. "Quinn, stop!" he shouted.

"Thanks but no thanks, Anthony," Quinn said without stopping. He bounded onto the roof and began to run. He could hear Anthony following him. He had to play it smart. Anthony was too strong to fool with. Quinn veered to the left, towards the door leading down off the roof. As Anthony lunged for him, he ran up the side of the structure and flipped, coming down behind the other man. Quinn shot forward, tackling Anthony through the door and into the stairwell beyond. They hit the wall in a tangle. Quinn shoved free and stepped back, slamming the door and sliding his cane through the handle, jamming it.

Anthony struck the door like a bull, rattling it on its hinges. Quinn took the opportunity to move to the other side of the roof and push himself off. He caught a window ledge and swung towards the nearby drain pipe, shimmying down into the courtyard below. Dropping lightly to the street, he pressed himself against the wall and peered around the corner. There was no sign of the Rolls-Royce. The sound of splintering wood echoed off the brick as Quinn stepped out of the alleyway and hailed a cab.

Anthony stumbled back out into the light, cursing a blue streak. Tom Gentry struggled up onto the roof a moment later, a Winchester Rifle clutched in one hand. "Did he get away?" he bellowed.

"Of course," Anthony said, stretching slightly.

"What? You expected him to?"

"Suspected might be a better word." Anthony turned, head tilted up. He sniffed the air slightly.

"You going to track him?" Tom said, gesturing to Anthony's nose.

Anthony blinked. "Now why would I do that? I know exactly where he's going, and when he's going to be there. Even as I planned."

Tom frowned. "Then what was with the damn pantomime in the car back there?"

Anthony tapped the side of his head. "Super-Detective, remember?"

Two blocks away and breathing heavily, Quinn lay back after giving directions to the cab driver. He ran a hand through his sweat-slick hair. This made three times he'd chosen the better part of valor when confronting Anthony. It was becoming a habit, one that grated on his confidence like steel on stone.

When he reunited with them, Silk put words to the feeling. "This stinks." The little man sat on the hood of the coup, smoking a cigarette. They were parked near the river, eating a late lunch.

"I'm telling you, guy ain't human," Butch said around a mouthful of cheese-steak sandwich.

"He's human enough. Just more experienced at this than us," Quinn said, loosening his tie. He'd bandaged his hands and cheek where his flesh had met the street. "But for a man as annoying as he's becoming, Mr. Anthony isn't all bad." He watched a pair of gulls cut the air over the water. "He's given us a fair bit of help so far. I hope he doesn't hold me kicking him out the car against me."

"Oh yeah, that's nothing to get worked up over," Silk said. "Guy can't hold a grudge for that."

"Glad you see it my way," Quinn said, without a hint of irony. "What do you know about this penthouse?" he continued.

Kirby, who had an almost encyclopedic knowledge of the underworld thanks to his time as an active part of it, frowned. "Penthouse? That's likely the Shandor Building. The Gentleman likes to move around a lot."

"He's paranoid is what I hear," Butch said.

"That too," Silk said. He held up several fingers and ticked them off. "He's got a place upstate, one in Jersey, one in Queens, and the Shandor Building. If he's in the city, it's likely that last one."

Quinn rubbed his chin. "What are the odds that Anthony knows that?" Both Silk and Butch gave him a look. Quinn raised his hands, chuckling. "Fair enough. So I need to get there first."

"Might I ask why?" Silk said. He took off his hat and scrubbed his fingers over his oiled scalp. "If Anthony and his people know, and they're just waiting until everyone is in the net, then why don't we do as he advised and back off?"

Quinn took a breath. Then, he said, "I can't." He looked at his associates. "It's not enough that I'm cleared. The Black Bat has to be shown to take care of his own business. To not be worried about the crooks or the cops or even Super-Detectives." He pounded a fist into his palm. "If I go to ground now, what will happen the next time I try to intimidate some stool-pigeon?"

"So...it's about pride then?" Silk said.

"No. It's about the job. Just like always," Quinn said. He took off his glasses, exposing his scarred features. "Come on gentlemen. We have a siege to prepare for."

The two former criminals looked at each other. "Siege?" Butch said.

"If I'm right, Pisco intends to kill the Gentleman tonight. I intend to be there when he tries, even if I have to shoot my way from the ground-floor up," Quinn said.

"You're lucky I brought your toys with me," Silk said, frowning. He hopped off the car and circled around it, popping the trunk. He opened the hidden compartment in the trunk lid and removed Quinn's costume and equipment harness. Then, he pulled out a second, small bandolier of pouches. He tossed the latter to his employer. "Gas pellets and flare caps." Silk tossed a shotgun to Butch, who checked its load briskly. "O'Leary and I will be armed more conventionally, I'm afraid."

"That's fine, because you're not going in with me," Quinn said.

"What?" Silk said.

"But Boss ..." Butch began.

Quinn held up a hand. "No buts. This is for me, and me alone." He smiled grimly. "Besides, I have a feeling I'm going to need a quick getaway after everything is said and done tonight."

There was little else to say. As the sun set, Quinn doffed his street-clothes and slid into the skin of the Black Bat. He strapped on his harness, the twin automatics resting beneath his arms, and then strapped the bandolier belt around his waist. He slid into the coup. "Let's go."

Silk pulled the car off the street a few blocks away from the Shandor Building. He turned slightly. "Want us to circle the block?"

"Keep it slow. Anthony will likely have the cops out in force. If it smells fishy, head home. I'll find my own way," the Black Bat said, climbing out through the opening in the roof. Crouching for a moment, he looked down at both Kirby and O'Leary. "Stay safe."

"You too Boss," O'Leary said, as the Black Bat disappeared into the night.

The Black Bat moved slowly across the rooftops, his senses strained to their utmost. He was wary of another trap, ready to run at the slightest noise. But he neither heard nor saw anything.

The Shandor Building rose up off of the edge of Central Park like a blotch of concrete and off-angle calculations. It looked like the kind of place a man like Gentleman Jack Schultz would find comfortable.

The penthouse was a dome of glass and steel that surmounted the spire of the building like a blister. Quinn frowned as he crouched, studying it. He looked down at the street, wondering how he ought to handle things. Despite his earlier bravado, he knew that tonight was going to be potentially more dangerous than any other night of his-what had Anthony called it?-his 'shadow-career'.

The police on one side, the criminals on the other, and in the middle, as usual, the Black Bat.

Pushing the thought aside, he looked at the time piece strapped to the underside of his wrist. Twenty to eight, and all was quiet. He could see shapes moving in the penthouse. He plucked a pair of miniature binoculars from within his harness and focused in on the penthouse. Silently, he counted seven men, plus a lean figure he knew to be the Gentleman. Copernick was there as well, finger-splints and all.

The Black Bat straightened slightly, resting on his heels as he considered how to go about things. Below, a car pulled up in front of the building, and a shape stepped out.

Pisco.

No backup, however. Either he was extremely confident, or something was up. The Black Bat frowned beneath his mask. Pisco didn't strike him as the type to take risks.

Figures darted across the street, keeping to the shadows. The Black Bat smiled. That was it. Pisco had set up a raid. Maybe he'd done it two nights ago as well. What better cover for a mole, than a raid? He'd set it up to draw out Leonardi, who'd paid the price with his life. Now, it was the Gentleman's turn.

All so Pisco could keep his badge and his pension and his pastrami sandwiches with McGrath. The Black Bat's smile faded like a morning mist. In its place was something altogether more unpleasant.

Was this what Anthony had meant about interfering? Had Anthony known that Pisco would do this? And if he had-what? The Black Bat shook his head in irritation.

Despite what he'd said before, he wasn't really a detective. Not as such. Too much brawn and not enough brains. He stood and spread his arms, letting the wind catch at his glider wings.

There was something to be said for the direct approach.

He pushed off and let the air take him, whipping him across the gap between his perch and the Shandor Building. Stretching his arms out, he narrowly hooked a handy gargoyle and curled around the dog-face demon, plucking himself out of the wind's grip. Then he began to climb, hand over hand, the thin steel hooks set into the palms of his gloves and the toes of his boots digging into the stone.

As he climbed, Leonardi's face came back to him, pale and splashed with crimson. Wide eyes, full of shock and surprise. He remembered the sound the badge had made, raising sparks as it sped across the floor.

The penthouse was a blossom of glass, supported by ingeniously bent girders and concrete pillars. The Black Bat slithered up onto a jutting spike of concrete and hunched for a moment, his eyes easily piercing the gloom and the glass to see the men within.

The Gentleman was there, dressed in a satin dressing gown, his narrow silver head nodding in time to the music echoing out of the radio set into the wall of the sitting room. His men stood at attention around the room, their eyes on Pisco even as he stepped out of the private elevator.

The Gentleman spread his arms in welcome as Pisco came to meet him. Pisco kept his head down and his arms at his sides. The Black Bat crept forward, drawing a pistol.

The glass was too thick to hear through, but the Black Bat wasn't concerned. He already knew what he needed to know. Now he was just waiting to interrupt the show. Gunshots sounded below, and a window shattered.

McGrath had likely jumped the gun again.

The men in the penthouse reacted predictably, some of them heading for the door, the others hustling the Gentleman towards the elevator. Pisco reached out and grabbed Schultz. Guns were drawn and the Black Bat knew he'd waited long enough.

He pulled his other pistol and fired both into the closest of the great petal-like windows, shattering it. Then he charged through, throwing himself to the floor even as the Gentleman's guards reacted to this new threat. Pistols snarled, slinging wads of lead towards the black-clad vigilante, who responded in kind.

Firing to keep their heads down, he holstered a pistol and then ripped a handful of smoke pellets off of his harness, hurling them randomly. With the window broken, the smoke would disperse quickly, but it would help while it lasted. He moved through it as his opponents gagged and coughed, momentarily blinded.

Two of the guards staggered as the Black Bat snuffed the life from them with well-placed shots. Another put a lucky shot across the Bat's bow, clipping him on the arm and causing him to spin, his automatic blazing. With his wounded arm, he fumbled a flare pellet into his hand and bounced it off the wall. Men yelped as they were blinded. Quinn pulled his second pistol and fired, cutting their affliction short.

A chair crashed across his back, nearly sending him to his knees and he bent, driving his foot into his attacker's belly. The man crumpled, wheezing, and the Black Bat stepped past him, spinning him into his comrades' line of fire. The smoke was clearing faster than he'd anticipated and as he stood a bullet cut a red trail across his forehead. The Black Bat staggered, blinded by the sudden gush of blood. Another bullet skidded across the meat of his thigh, nearly toppling him and causing him to drop his weapons.

"You're dead!" Copernick howled, firing again, the bullet gouging splinters out of the floor. The Black Bat lunged for him, grappling with the other man. Copernick screamed as the Black Bat grabbed his broken fingers and bent them back. As the gunsel jerked away, the Black Bat drove the stiffened fingers of his free hand into the other man's throat. Trachea crushed, Copernick sank to his knees, gagging. The Black Bat, half-blind, dove through an open doorway as a Thompson opened up, chewing away at the plaster and Copernick both.

"Give it up, freak," a smooth voice said. "You're done." The Gentleman. It couldn't be anyone else.

"I decide when I'm done, Schultz," the Black Bat said, pushing himself up along the wall. "Not you. In fact, you don't get to decide anything anymore."

"Who says? You?" the Gentleman retorted. The Thompson roared again, cutting a line of black ruptures through the wall and sending the Black Bat scrambling. He crouched, searching wildly. He caught sight of one of his pistols, laying not far away.

"The cops are probably right outside your door, Schultz," the Black Bat called. "They're on their way in. And you're on your way out."

The Thompson fired again and the Black Bat moved, sliding on his belly across the floor towards his pistol. His hand stretched out, his fingers reaching. His skin crawled as he felt the Gentleman swing the Thompson towards him. He grabbed the gun and shot to his feet, turning. Too late. He was going to be too late.

Time seemed to slow down as he swung the pistol around and stared down the barrel of the Thompson. The Gentleman smiled nastily. "You can come out Pisco. I got him."

"Yeah?" Pisco said, stepping out from where he'd been hiding. "If you hold him, we can probably swing this ..."

"Swing what? You bringing in your buddies in blue?" The Gentleman's eyes were like ice and Pisco took a step back as they caught him. "Don't look so surprised. Once a rat, always a rat," the Gentleman said. He stepped back, swinging the Thompson. "No. No, I can kill two birds with one bullet. I can shut you up, Pisco. And I can get the Bat out of my hair."

"You won't get away with this," Pisco said. The Gentleman laughed.

"He's right," the Black Bat said harshly. "I'm not just going to let you shoot me, Schultz." He raised the automatic. "The Black Bat won't go down quietly."

"Quiet or loud, I'm willing to take the risk," the Gentleman said. "Goodbye, boys."

The Bat steeled himself for a death-leap. There was no way he could avoid the spray of the gun, but he might be able to take the Gentleman with him. He glanced at Pisco, who seemed to have the same idea. Then the crooked cop went one way, and the Bat dove the other and the Thompson howled.

The Black Bat rolled across the floor, the Thompson tracking him with deadly precision. And then, suddenly, it choked to a stop. The Black Bat sprang up, pistol raised.

Pisco stood over the Gentleman, holding the Thompson by its barrel. He tossed it down as the Bat stood. "Nick of time, Mr. Quinn."

The Black Bat blinked. Pisco grinned and straightened, looking suddenly more bulky than the Black Bat remembered. He reached up and peeled away portions of his face as the Bat watched, revealing the olive features of Jim Anthony beneath.

"Anthony?" the Black Bat said in disbelief.

"None other," Anthony said, tossing his disguise onto the chest of the unconscious gentleman. "I apologize for not getting more directly involved, but I didn't want to endanger this beauty." He opened his shirt and revealed a compact tape recorder and microphone attached to his chest with flesh-colored tape.

"You got a confession?"

"I got enough to make the charges stick this time," Anthony said. He cocked his head, as if listening. The Black Bat heard it as well-the saturnine bellow of McGrath on the warpath. "You had best go."

"You're letting me go? Just like that?"

"I said that I had no intention of bringing you in and I meant it,"

Anthony said.

"But you never said why?"

Anthony sighed. "I didn't, did I? Like as not, Mr. Quinn, you're the future."

"Don't sound so happy about it."

"I'm not. But I'm pragmatic enough to accept it. The day of gentleman adventurers is coming to a close, I think. It's time for a new breed of extra-legal operator." He looked at the Black Bat. "Men like you, Mr. Quinn. Men like the Black Bat."

The Black Bat was silent, not knowing quite how to reply. Anthony looked around the room, frowning, then back at the Bat. "Go before I change my mind, Mr. Quinn."

The Black Bat nodded brusquely. "Good working with you, Mr. Anthony."

"Call me Jim," Anthony said, saluting him lazily.

"Yeah," the Black Bat said, stepping to the window. "Maybe someday." And then he was gone. Anthony waited a moment, then two, before turning to the door to summon McGrath and the others.

And behind him, wings spread, the Black Bat rode the night wind to freedom.

The End

'When Titans Clash'

So, why pit the Black Bat against Jim Anthony, you might ask. To which I'd certainly reply, well, why not? The 'fight-n-team-up' is a (theoretically) beloved cliché of heroic fiction for a reason, you know. Gilgamesh fought Enkidu, Batman fought Superman and Doc Savage has tangled with the Shadow on at least two occasions. Titans clash. That's what they do.

The key is you have to make the reason that they do so a good one. I picked a dependable old standby, the false accusation, and involved the Super-Detective to ferret out the truth in one way, while the Black Bat sought it in his own inimitable fashion. Of course, despite both of them being nominally on the same side, there'd have to be a confrontation or two.

Since I was writing from the Bat's perspective, however, the story offered an interesting opportunity to show just what fighting a man like Jim Anthony (or Doc Savage) would be like for someone who's not superhuman in some regard.

Still, it's the old 'who'd win' argument, pulp-style. The Black Bat possesses super-senses, some neat gimmicks and those twin automatics that he employs so freely. Jim Anthony, on the other hand, is very nearly super-human and has more than a few gimmicks of his own. It's an even match-up, as far as I can see, though, since this is a Black Bat story and not a Jim Anthony story, I tried to give the former a victory of sorts, even if it was only a moral one.

I'll leave it up to you to say whether I succeeded or not.

JOSH REYNOLDS - is a freelance writer of moderate skill and exceptional confidence. He has written a bit, and some of it was even published. For money. By real people. His work has appeared in anthologies such as *Historical Lovecraft*, and in periodicals such as *Innsmouth Magazine* and *Hammer & Bolter*.

Feel free to stop by his blog, [http://joshuamreynolds.blogspot.com/] to check up on him or to tell him he's wrong about whatever it is you disagree with him about.

A Black Bat Adventure

by
Jim Beard

As summer waned and fall marched closer, the people of Queensburg were learning to fear sundown. Nighttime brought fear, fear in the form of enemy airplanes overhead. That was peculiar in itself, but more so in the fact that the country was not at war. Not yet, at least.

The other peculiar thing was that Queensburg was a small, sleepy town that lay along the Hudson River, just about eighty or so miles north of New York City. As such, it wasn't exactly the kind of place to write home about concerning its strategic importance. With a population of didn't much impress a congressman and the kind of quiet, up-state charm one might expect, it just didn't seem the kind of place that would have become a hotbed of terror.

Regardless, its citizens were scared. And they did and said nothing about it.

As this quiet conundrum began to unfold, came two men, motoring on their way from Rochester to the Big Apple. A wholly-unexpected flat tire had laid them low and they stopped in Queensburg for repairs and maybe a bite to eat. As the men made their tired way across an empty street and into a relatively cheerful looking diner, the sun was dropping into the west.

"Here," said the one man to the other. "This looks like an okay place to stop."

The speaker was a hulking mountain of man wrapped up tight in a large, black coat. He had to duck slightly to enter through the door of the diner. Grunting a weak approval as he got an eyeful of the place, the giant turned to his compatriot.

"I've seen better and I've seen worse. But, we got no choice, I guess."

"No," answered the other man. "Not really. Let's get a table and we can ask about borrowing a tire iron. Better make it look like you're guiding me in for a landing, Butch."

The giant's accomplice was no midget himself. Tall and roughly handsome, his black, wavy hair matched his own coat - and the dark glasses that rested over his eyes. To the diner's customers, it appeared as if the man was blind. The man-mountain's hand on his friend's arm to lead him to a table seemed to confirm this.

But the stranger wasn't blind at all; in fact, his sight far exceeded that of anyone in the diner at that time, or possibly anyone in the entire country, for that matter.

Tony Quinn had been making steady progress as a crusading District Attorney when a splash of acid from reckless criminals severely impeded his career path. Though blinded by the corrosive and sporting hideous scars like bracelets around his eyes, the young man could not reconcile his new sightlessness with his fervent desire to bring justice to the people. Several conferences with the world's most proficient medical specialists later, his personal picture of the future appeared more than dim.

Then, when the night looked its blackest, a woman approached him with an amazing offer: her murdered father's eyes and the possibility of sight. The miraculous operation that followed blessed Tony with not only restored vision, but, somehow, a level of unearthly visual acuity that allowed him to operate in that blackest night as well as the brightest day.

Tony Quinn, now working as a mere lawyer, was more than what he seemed. He decided to continue to present a blind face to the world, but, for his own purposes, also continued to mete out justice to those who needed it the most.

After getting settled in a booth, the young attorney glanced around the diner. He made sure so as not to turn his head while doing so, lest he look as though his blindness was a sham.

From his vantage point – Butch had chosen a spot where they could see almost the entire diner – Tony saw at least four customers, plus a waitress. In addition, he also spotted two young children peering around the front counter, near the cash register, doing a very poor job of not being curious about the newcomers.

Two men sat in another booth on the other side of the room. One was a wiry sort, with longish locks and a sort-of hungry look. He was speaking animatedly, yet in low tones, to a nondescript older gentlemen seated across from him. That personage was dressed up in a suit and tie and, for some reason, still wearing his hat. He nodded occasionally at the thin man, cold and impassive.

Another man sat on a stool by himself at the counter. He was also sharply-dressed, but with finer clothes than the man in the booth, and currently nursing a cup of coffee. In front of him sat an orphaned piece of pie, half-eaten.

At a table at the far side of the room perched a lady of perhaps forty or forty-five years. Though her face hung down over what looked like a magazine, Tony caught the quick, bird-like glances she made in his and Butch's direction. He wasn't surprised; they were strangers and it was getting late. He didn't know much about Queensburg at all, he realized, save for its general geographic location and, if the nearby buildings did not lie, its apparently vintage age.

The waitress approached their booth and smiled. It was a tight smile that spoke of a weary, long day. She sported a pad and a pencil. Tony, looking out of the corners of his eyes and keeping his head pointed in Butch's direction, noticed her wedding band and her short, un-lacquered nails.

"Gentlemen, can I get you anything? Coffee? Some food?"

She was very pretty, but Tony could see some premature aging in her auburn hair and around her green eyes. She worried a lot, he guessed. Her voice was strained, too.

"Ah," began Tony, turning in her direction. "Thank you very much. We'll both have coffee, please. Also, could you tell me – is there a mechanic's garage nearby?"

The waitress frowned. Tony made no notice of her expression, keeping his own expression in check. "Well, yes, but…its getting late and…what do you…I'm sorry, I'm being rude." She looked back and forth between Tony and Butch. "The garage would be closed at this time, I'm afraid. Is it terribly important?"

Something ticked the back of Tony's skull, in the part of his brain that sensed trouble. It wasn't a four-alarmer, but it put him in a slightly-higher degree of awareness, a higher level than that in which he normally existed. Butch noticed it, too; he was sure of it.

"We had a flat," said the giant. "Out on the main drag. Got a spare in the trunk, but *someone* forgot to pack a tire iron."

Tony smiled. "Now, now, Butch – Silk's normally a very efficient man, and not prone to forget things. Though, I must admit, his forgetfulness is hard to forgive this time."

Silk Kirby acted as Tony's chauffeur back in New York. A good man, he also toiled as the attorney's eyes and ears in certain rougher quarters of the underworld. He was currently escorting Carol Baldwin on an important errand in the city, leaving Butch O'Leary to act as driver for Tony's mission to Rochester on behalf of a client. It was Carol's father whose eyes now rested in the lawyer's noggin.

"Well," said the waitress slowly, reluctantly. "I guess I could call Mr. Mellicon and see if he's still up. He lives above his garage, you see."

"That would be greatly appreciated," replied Tony "If it's not too much of an inconvenience, miss…?"

"Tobin. Sarah Tobin. I own the Redcoat Diner. And its 'Mrs.,' though I'm a widow…"

"Mrs. Tobin, then," said Tony with a smile. "Thank you very much. You have a very nice place. We don't wish to make any extra work for anyone, just hoping to borrow a tire iron so Mr. O'Leary here can replace the tire and we can be on our way."

The waitresses smiled slightly back, but an air of tension still hung upon her. Tony wondered what was eating at her. It seemed to him as if his and Butch's presence was causing her undue apprehension.

"We'll try to get you right back on the road, sir," she said. "I'll bring you your coffees…on the house."

Before Tony could tell the woman that wasn't necessary, the thin man across the room called out her name. She spun on her heel and with a strange, quick look back at Tony and Butch, she zipped off to attend to her other customers.

"Something," began the lawyer, "is up."

"You noticed that, too, huh?" grunted Butch. He sighed and looked out the window at the setting sun, its colors suddenly ominous, not pretty. "Great. That's just great. Another mystery. And me without my boxing gloves."

Tony Quinn grinned at this old friend's words, knowing full well the ex-prizefighter lived for a fight – and too often got one while playing bodyguard for his "sightless" boss. Butch had once been a true master of the ring and a devotee of the so-called "sweet science," but a crooked deal with mobsters to throw a bout curtailed his pugilistic practice. Thankfully, he found all the action he craved at Tony's side.

"I'm not so sure that I'm ready to believe that little Queensburg's a den of iniquity and vice just yet, Butch, but Mrs. Tobin is acting awfully queer about something. Something, unless I miss my guess, about how late it's getting. Did you notice, too, that she kept glancing out the window as she talked with us?"

Butch O'Leary had to admit he didn't notice that bit of action, but he certainly noticed that Sarah Tobin was a looker. "Hate to see a pretty thing like that all nervous, Tony. It wounds me right here." He patted his chest over his heart.

"Hmm," breathed the young man. "She seems to be arguing with the well-heeled gentlemen at the counter at the moment."

"That's Mr. Conklin," said a small, quiet voice next to Tony Quinn. "He's a big dummy."

Tony turned to see a young, eight-year-old boy standing by his side, looking at him with wide eyes and a slightly sullen expression. Behind him hid an even younger little girl, shy yet very curious about the men. It was the two children he eyeballed when he and Butch first came in.

"I'm afraid I don't know him well enough to call him a dummy," said Tony to the boy. "Perhaps you can tell me why you think he is."

Before the boy could reply, the little girl poked her head out. "Why's he wearing those big dark glasses, Danny?" She spoke with all the innocence, all the naivety, of a child.

Danny turned to her, annoyed. "'Cause he's *blind*, Sam. That's why. Geez!" The boy turned back to Tony, somewhat embarrassed. "Sorry, mister. She's just a little kid."

"My name is Samantha," squeaked the girl, still almost fully behind her brother.

Tony leaned back a bit, in an attempt to not frighten the girl with his dark glasses. He touched the frames with one hand, to make certain they were sitting squarely on his face and fully covering the deep scarring that lay beneath them.

"It's a very pretty name," Tony said to the girl. "I hope you will allow me to introduce myself and my friend. I am Mr. Quinn, and this is Mr. O'Leary. We're strangers to your town and we're just stopping here briefly to see about getting a tire on our motorcar fixed."

"You better get it done soon," grimaced Danny. "Before the planes come."

Butch O'Leary started, jumped a bit in his seat. "What th'..." spat Butch, but Tony laid a hand on his friend's arm. He hoped the children hadn't noticed how unerring his aim had been with that movement.

"I'm sorry," said Tony, keeping his voice calm and his face friendly. "What do you mean, Danny, when you say 'planes'?"

Over the heads of the children, he saw their mother – Tony guessed they were Sarah's kids – still locked in discussion with Mr. Conklin at the counter. The other woman and the other two men were also still in their same places. Everything seemed relatively calm, but again he felt a thin, electric wire of tension running straight through the diner. He couldn't place it, get his arms around it.

"The planes," answered Danny in a clear voice. "The ones that come at night. We heard 'em for, I think, three nights now? Lots of people are kinda scared by 'em, but *I'm* not. Well, not much, I guess..."

Tony sighed inwardly. He and Butch were on their way back to New York after escorting a client to Rochester, a client who severely needed his help. He was glad to do it, not just because the young woman was his client, but because she was someone in need. It was as simple as that. Here now, if he was sizing up the situation as he felt it was revealing itself, was another case of need. Tony was sure of it, though he could neither define it nor put an accurate name to it at the moment.

Before he could continue to question the children, another piece of the puzzle presented itself.

The door to the Redcoat Diner flew open. Three men burst in. The door sprang back after it hit the wall and nearly into the face of the first man. He caught it, angrily, and stared around the diner, taking everyone in with his piercing gaze.

"Get those lights out, Sarah! *Now*, woman!" he bellowed.

Tony took in the men's scruffy appearance, in contrast to the patrons of the diner. While not exactly bums or indigents, the men were obviously working-class and not accustomed to regular bathing or shaving. One of them smelled particularly strong of a distinctive odor, a bit of information that Tony's keen sense of smell caught and recorded. He couldn't quite place it, though it was familiar to him.

The tension in the diner escalated within the space of seconds.

Sarah Tobin rushed right up to the first man as the other two squeezed in around him and made their way towards the patrons. Planting herself squarely in front of the man, the diner owner threw up her hands as if to ward him off.

"Now, you hold it right there, John Tulane," she hissed. "I told you before – you do *not* come in *my* place and try to scare *my* customers with your damn foolishness!"

The man grabbed the woman's wrists. Butch shifted in his seat, began to rise. Tony's hand shot own once more and gripped at his bodyguard's sleeve. "Wait," he said under his breath. "Let this play out for another beat or two."

"Sarah, I *told* you! The planes can see the lights! Gotta put 'em out or they can spot you *easily*!"

Samantha began to cry. The female diner patron started to squawk a bit, not unlike a disturbed heron. The man with the longish hair began to stand up himself and open his mouth as if to protest. His fellow diner, the man with the hat, remained impassive.

Then came the sound of planes.

Everyone froze, as if in tableau. Tony Quinn looked over at Butch O'Leary and saw the confusion that came over the man-mountain's face. The attorney had seen and heard many strange things in his young life, but his older friend had experienced even more. Tony could tell immediately that Butch had never really encountered something this queer before.

Suddenly, little Danny Tobin spoke up.

"They're here! They're here!" he yelled, his calm now shattered by intense fright. "They're gonna drop *bombs* on us! Just like Mr. Tulane said, Mom!"

His sister wailed. Tulane threw Sarah to the floor and one of his fellows smashed the main ceiling lights.

The diner was plunged into deep, inky darkness and the drone of the planes grew louder.

Tony Quinn decided the situation was about as surreal as he had ever experienced. Stuck in a darkened diner in a little upstate New York town, with what seemed to be an entire squadron of airplanes right over his head.

The drone of the engines began softly, but grew swiftly and in a moment grew to healthy proportions. There was no mistaking the sound. What he couldn't figure was the why of it.

Tony patted Butch on the shoulder. The touch told the big man that his boss was on the move. The young attorney slunk across the darkened floor of the diner and towards the door. With his amazing vision, all the little restaurant's patrons could be clearly seen in various states.

He side-stepped around one of the rough men who'd barged their way in when the planes were approaching, slipped around the bird-like woman and sidled up to the door. Tony doubted very much that he had been heard, so soft was his tread. Years of experience were behind his movements.

Near the door, the man called Tulane crouched on the floor. Near him sat Sarah Tobin, shaking from what Tony assumed to be anger, rather than fear. He stepped around them both and reached for the handle of the door. It squeaked when he turned it and the door stuck a little when he pulled it open.

"Hey!" blurted out Tulane. "Don't go out there!"

Tony ignored him. Opening the door, he took a tentative step over the threshold and stuck his head and shoulders outside. He listened.

The sound of the droning plane engines was everywhere. Tony could determine no exact point of origin or direction. It filled the air with a heavy cloak of unceasing weight and substance. It was maddening, not being able to pinpoint its location.

The lawyer looked up, saw nothing. Around him, the street was darkened, as well as all the windows of the buildings in the immediate area. Someone had been thorough with the blackout.

A trickle of anger crept into Tony's demeanor. The sound of the planes offended him on some deep level, a place where his pride of country resided. The United States was not at war, though overseas the promise of it grew like a cancer. He couldn't imagine that the planes could be those of the U.S. Army Air Force or even the Coast Guard – he had never heard of them flying so low and in such force directly over a city or town. And, if it was to be believed, for several nights. But if some other country was behind it, how would they have gotten past the US defenses?

Before he could ponder the mystery any further, a hand clamped down on his shoulder and pulled him back inside the diner.

"Who are you?" shouted the owner of the hand. "What do you think you're doing?" It was the rough-around-the-edges man called Tulane.

Before Tony could respond or react, a giant man-mountain stepped up behind Tulane, laid one massive hand on the man's shoulder and with the other flipped open a cigarette lighter. A small flame flared into life from it, illuminating the surroundings.

"Buddy," said Butch O'Leary in a calm, controlled and all-together menacing voice. "You better remove that claw of yours from my boss, or I swear you're gonna lose it."

Tony stood his ground. Tulane looked back and forth from Tony to Butch and then, finally, released Tony. His arm slumped down to his side and he turned to face Butch.

"Okay, mister. We don't want no trouble. Its just that this guy here was gonna put us all in danger, see?"

"What danger?" ejaculated Tony. The sound of the planes was now fading, he realized. "From those planes? Whose are they? Where are they from? Why would you say we were in danger from them?"

Tulane looked sheepishly at the attorney. "Listen, Mister – you can see how scared everyone is here. It's the planes. They get everybody all crazy. Me and my friends, we just make sure everyone's safe – can't you see that?"

Tony mightily resisted the urge to point out to the man that he was blind – or at least that was the story he presented to the world. He started to speak, but was interrupted from a feminine, yet strong, voice.

"I think you'd better leave now, Mr. Tulane," said Sarah Tobin, firmly. "I'll inform the sheriff tomorrow about what happened here."

"Yeah, well maybe I'll be talking to him *first* – c'mon, boys."

And with that, the three thugs were gone, leaving behind them several people; some of them scared, some of them angry and some of them very confused.

Sarah Tobin reached out and silently asked Butch for the loan of his lighter. He obliged and watched as she picked her way over to the counter. She bent down behind it and then produced two lanterns, which she preceded to light. The new illumination cast strange and garish shadows on the wall, adding to the overall singular weirdness of the situation.

Tony heard sniffling and looked over to see Danny and Samantha Tobin with tears in their eyes and morose expressions on their young faces. Sarah clucked and rushed over to them. Enveloping the children in her arms, she led them to a booth and made them sit down.

The well-dressed man from the counter cleared his throat and spoke to no one in particular.

"Well," he said, shaking his head. "Welcome to Queensburg."

Butch cut through the awkwardness of the moment. "What the hell is goin' on here, anyway?"

"I think I'll just go, Sarah," said the bird-woman suddenly. "My money's on the table."

"Yes, goodnight, Mrs. Marsh. I'm sorry about all the fuss. I hope you'll come back tomorrow."

The woman left. Tony stepped forward, careful to make it seem as if his blindness was making everything seem even more confusing. He turned in the general direction of Sarah Tobin and the man, Conklin.

"Forgive us, but we're obviously strangers here and have no idea what to make of all this," he said. "My name is Quinn. I'm an attorney from New York City. This is my associate, Mr. O'Leary. Now that we're properly introduced, may we be told what the deuce just happened?"

The well-dressed man walked over to Tony and offered his hand, then realized his mistake. "I'm Frank Conklin. I own a business here in town. The Redcoat Diner is one of my favorite places to eat. I hope you won't think we're being too inhospitable, Mr. Quinn…"

Sarah started to say something, but the long-haired man – Tony had almost forgotten about him – cut in abruptly.

"It's only your favorite place to eat," he began sharply and in a high-pitched voice. "Because you're trying to buy the diner from Mrs. Tobin! That's all you ever think about, Conklin – money, money, money!"

Frank Conklin wheeled around angrily on the man, his face beginning to redden and his cheeks puffing out. He looked for all the world like a bantam hen; Tony thought that at any second he'd start scratching the floor with his feet and begin squawking.

"Shut *up*, Severn," said Conklin. "Keep your long nose out of my business. I can do and say anything I want. That's all between Sarah and myself."

Tony was gifted immediately with a rapidly-expanding picture of the relationship between the three people who stood before him. He saw greed, avarice, pride, jealousy and, yes, a bit of fright. But, it told him absolutely nothing about the planes.

"Gentlemen, please," pleaded Sarah Tobin. "I am standing right here and I don't wish to be spoken about as if I'm not. Now, it's late and we've all had a…well, we all need to be heading home and to our beds. Please see yourselves out."

The man named Severn sniffed loudly. "Oh, I'm leaving. Your prices are much too high, anyway, Sarah Tobin. You shut out the common man on the street with such exclusivity."

"I suppose you'd like it better if everything here was free?" said Sarah, barely hiding the derision in her voice.

"He would indeed," offered Frank Conklin. "His kind is always looking for a hand-out. Better not forget your books, Mr. Teacher – must be ready tomorrow to fill young minds with your…well, I was going to say 'clap-trap,' but I'll be kind and say simply 'knowledge'."

The long-haired educator sniffed again and stalked back to his booth, grabbed up what appeared to be a stack of books and notepads, and stomped out the door. Tony noticed his threadbare pants and patched-at-the-elbows coat as he flew from the diner.

Conklin shook his head and tipped his hat to Sarah. Wishing her a goodnight, he passed by Tony and Butch without so much as a farewell and was out the door himself.

That left just the man in the hat who had been keeping the company of the teacher. "That's just Mr. Stanwald," said Sarah. "He's a nice old sort. He's mute, some kind of injury from the War. Likes to sit and listen to anyone who'll talk to him. Don't pay him any mind – he'll come and go with no fanfare."

The lawyer turned to the diner owner. "Mrs. Tobin, please, tell us what's going on here in Queensburg?" He spread out his hands in an open gesture toward the sky, hoping he appeared sincere and non-threatening. Inside, Tony burned with the desire to get to the root of the problem.

"Why? Why would you care?"

Tony softly smiled. "Call me a…a hopeless do-gooder, ma'am. Butch and I would like to help, if only we knew what this was all about." He watched as the woman got out a broom and a dustpan and began to sweep. It seemed to Tony like an action calculated to keep her calm and focused.

"It's really…nothing. Nothing much at all," she began. "About two weeks ago, we first heard the sounds – the planes, I guess. No one thought much about it. They didn't sound *close*, not like now. But…there were a few people who got a bit riled up."

"Mr. Drovik started going on and on!" yelped Danny, who had left his booth and had suddenly appeared by Tony's side. "He said that it was a sign that the gov'ment was watching over us and…and a whole buncha other stuff!"

"Severn Drovik, you met him tonight," Sarah noted. "I'm afraid he can become very excitable at times. Has a lot of funny notions." A puzzled look fell over her countenance.

"Anyway," she continued, "after that first time, Sheriff Kent came around and talked with everyone, said there was no cause for alarm, that he thought it was just some military exercises and that we should remain calm. I thought that was odd, because, for the most part, everyone *was* calm already. Then, it happened again. Two, maybe three nights later, we heard the planes, but they were closer sounding. A few more people got a bit concerned. Next day, Mr. Tulane comes around with his friends and, well, starts riling everybody up some. Saying how he knows the sound of airplane engines well and that was no American engines – that they were *foreign* aircraft."

"Mr. Conklin tol' him he was crazy!" added Danny. "Said that no way at all could there be any enemy airplanes over our fair and sacred soil!"

Butch O'Leary glanced over at Tony, perhaps trying to gauge his boss' expression, his thoughts. On the surface, it *was* crazy. There was trouble in Europe, of course, but America wasn't involved in that. Not yet. No, it sounded insane, all right, but Butch credited himself a fair judge of character and he didn't think that Sarah had any reason to tell tall tales.

Foreign aircraft flying missions over upstate New York? Preposterous.

"I'm sorry, Mr....Quinn, was it?" asked Sarah Tobin. "It's very late now and I have to get this cleaned up and get these two very, very bad children to bed. And figure out how I'm going to get these lights fixed. Oh! And I didn't even call Mr. Mellicon about your tire iron. I'm terribly sorry!"

"But," insisted Tony. "I have many more questions, Mrs. Tobin. That's an incredible story, one that frankly would be hard to believe if I hadn't heard those planes with my own ears. Can't you tell me any more? Have they been getting closer? Does it seem as if more people are scared now? And what more has your sheriff said or done about it? Has anyone even called the nearest airbase and checked –"

Sarah Tobin planted one little fist on a hip and gestured with the broom. "Please, Mr. Quinn. It's late. You and your friend here need to be on your way, see? I think it would be best if you left. The garage is right down the street and then to your right at the first cross street. You can't miss it. Mr. Mellicon lives right up above it.

"Please...won't you just go?"

To Tony, the look on Sarah Tobin's face spoke volumes. But, he simply could not let her know he saw it, nor was swayed by it. He had to be consistent in his blindness act.

"The illuminations…cast strange…shadows on the wall…"

"Then, won't you just tell us," he said. "Is there is a hotel nearby?"

"No, no," Sarah admonished. "The hotel owner is…on vacation. There are no rooms to let at this time. Now, off you and your friend go."

The young attorney and his bodyguard did not protest further. With a curt bow and a tip of his hat, he let Butch lead the way out. As he went, Tony noticed that Mr. Stanwald had already left, apparently unbeknownst to all assembled.

The two men stepped onto the sidewalk and walked to the nearest corner. They stopped, tried to collect their thoughts. The darkened street, the silence, hung like an enigma all around them. They had no concrete answers to this enigma.

"Well," said Butch, "I figure we're surrounded by crazy people."

"You heard the planes the same as me," replied Tony.

"Well, I guess that makes us crazy, too."

Tony Quinn drew in a breath as he pulled closed his coat. "Here's what we know. Aircraft of unknown origin are flying over this town at somewhat regular intervals, always at night and for reasons unknown. We heard them. That's a fact. Some people are concerned, others are scared. Still others seem…involved, somehow. Those men, that Tulane, they have the stink of involvement on them. And this blackout – that doesn't just happen. That's control of a higher sort. I think that's where we need to start."

Butch O'Leary smiled to himself. This was his employer, his friend. There was no question that they wouldn't look into this, try to solve this mystery. And Butch knew that Tony Quinn had what it would take to crack this one.

They began to walk down the street, slowly, filled with thought.

"The people in that diner," offered Butch. "They were an offbeat bunch. That Sarah, a real nice dame and a looker, like I said, but she's gettin' nervous. Got those kids to think of. That Conklin? Bad news. That kind of mug throws bills around and thinks he owns the place. I just met him and I want to lay him out on the canvas. And that teacher? More bad news. His kind – well, I ain't got words for it. A real 'peaceful' type…but trouble."

"And quiet Mr. Stanwald?" asked the attorney. "What's your read on him, Butch?"

"No read, really. He ain't setting off any of my alarms. Feel kind of bad for him; I know other guys that were hurt in the War. Terrible, terrible stuff."

Tony took it all in, all of his bodyguard's words and opinions. There was much they didn't know. Pieces of the puzzle that weren't even on the table. They had little to go on.

Then, another piece presented itself.

Three dark forms materialized in front of them. They wore hoods over their heads and brandished pistols. The lead man motioned for Tony and Butch to enter the shadowy mouth of the alley from which they had just exited. There was little question as to what the men intended. Tony nodded slowly and unobtrusively to Butch as the man-mountain took his boss' arm and led him to the alley.

Therein, they were told to halt, to stand up against a wall. Around them, dark, almost-indistinguishable shapes were scattered around. To Tony, they were clear as day: a few crates, odds and ends of discarded detritus.

"We don't care much for strangers here," croaked the lead man. "Especially those who walk around at night."

"So, it's to be a robbery, then?" inquired Tony, calm and unperturbed. He stepped forward slightly, weighing the odds that his supposed-blindness would lure the men into a false sense of security. He decided to lay it on a bit thicker.

"Not very hospitable to the handicapped, I see. And here my friend and I were just saying what a nice town we had stumbled into."

The hooded man took a step towards Tony and jabbed the muzzle of his pistol into the young lawyer's chest. "Yeah, well, you ain't gonna be stumbling back *out*. You're going out in a box, pal…"

The sound of the wood slat that connected with the man's skull rang out like a gunshot in the small, darkened alley. The man staggered and went down on one knee, wailing. Tony dropped the slat and planted his own knee in the man's face. There was a sickening crunch.

Then, all hell broke loose.

Butch O'Leary charged forward like the prizefighter he was and landed a clean right hook on one of the other bandits. The man grunted and twirled around like a child's top. The third man took aim at the giant and fired. Butch was, fortunately, still in motion and not keen to present himself as a target. The bullet missed him by a half-inch.

Tony grabbed the man he had swatted and pulled him to his own level.

"I can't see you my friend, but I can hear you just fine." He punched him in the face. The man went down completely.

The ex-boxer grasped his opponent in two meaty paws and swung him like a hammer at the third man. Body slammed into body, the sound not unlike what could be heard at your average meatpackers. Grunts and groans issued forth.

In the middle of the fight, something niggled at the back of Tony's brain and he swung around to see a silhouette of a man at the mouth of the alley. The black form just stood there, like a statue. Tony could make out no features; nothing to identify the person. He wore a hood, like their assailants, and a heavy cloak or robe. The form exuded evil.

Suddenly, the two bandits who were still standing turned tail and ran in the opposite direction of the fourth man. Butch, exclaimed, "Hey!" and tore off after them.

Tony heard his friend's yell, turned to see what was happening. Before he could call Butch back, a heavy blow descended on the back of his skull. He was sure that one entire wall of the alley had fallen on him. He crumpled to the ground, stars exploding before his eyes. His dark glasses fell off. The earth twirled and danced. Tony felt vomit rise from his gullet.

He fell fully onto the dirty, garbage-strewn ground of the alley, his consciousness dancing away from him like a jilted lover. He fought to hold onto it. He snatched at it, feverishly. He thought he heard the sound of planes overhead. He also thought maybe he was already dead.

Everything went black then, as if he were blind. Truly blind.

A moment passed. Then two. Then a third. Something like consciousness came back to him for a short visit. Tony opened his eyes and looked up to see someone standing over him. The man wore a shiny badge.

"Well," said the man. "Good. You're under arrest, sir."

After awakening the next morning, Tony Quinn learned many things. Chief among them were that he sported a knot on the back of his head the size of a cantaloupe and that he was incarcerated in the Queensburg jail. His jailer introduced himself as Sheriff Martin Kent.

With a few cups of surprisingly good coffee in him, Tony listened through the bars of his little cell as Sheriff Kent laid out the situation and asked a few questions.

One, the young lawyer was being held on suspicion of public brawling and intoxication. Two, Butch O'Leary had returned too late from chasing one of the hooded thugs to rescue his boss from the long arm of the law. Three, no sign of the thugs – or their presumed leader – could be found. Tony argued that there was absolutely no evidence of intoxication to be able to hold him on such an accusation. The sheriff agreed.

"That just leaves the other accusation," pointed out Tony. "Either charge me with public brawling or let me go. Preferably let me go. Or find the real culprits."

Sheriff Kent stopped what he was doing and rounded on his prisoner. "Well," he said. "I suppose you do know the law, Mr. Quinn. But I know my town. And, though it's quite obvious, I am in charge of maintaining law and order in it. I'll thank you to let me handle things in my own way."

The man was, from what Tony could discern, in his late 50s or early 60s, not tall, but with a certain care-worn stature. Graying and lined, Sheriff Kent reminded him of an aging lawman from the Old West, sans the Hollywood cowboy accent. He took his job seriously, but was alone in his operations.

"My associate, Mr. O'Leary, will be coming back any moment now, to report on the fixing of our tire. It would be appreciated, very much so, if you could release me then. Or, as I said, simply charge me with a crime."

Sheriff Kent stared at the blind lawyer. Sized him up. If there was the possibility of a stare-down between the two men, most likely neither would have blinked. Finally, the sheriff reached up to rub his chin and turned away once again.

"Sheriff," implored Tony. "I just can't wrap my head around the fact that you don't seem to be doing much about these planes. Do you have any idea of what such an event might mean? And the attack on myself and Mr. O'Leary in the alley – is that normal for your town? You seem to be more concerned with paperwork and sweeping the floor than with catching criminals and protecting Queensburg."

"Let me tell you a few things, Mr. Quinn," Kent said. "About Queensburg. Did you know that it was almost the first capital of New York? Were you aware that the British burned it nigh to the ground, way back in 1778? Did you know that the people here don't care much for outsiders sticking their big city noses into their business? No, I am certain you do not know these things or many other things about this town.

"I believe I have your number, Mr. Quinn. You drive around, with your experiences in the big city tucked neatly under your belt and you think you know everything. Along comes what you determine to be a 'mystery' and you want to 'solve' it. You will not settle for anything less. You're what they call a 'crusading attorney,' aren't you? I call you a nuisance; someone who'd benefit from a bit of time *behind* bars himself, instead of sending others there. That's some experience I think even a blind man might find illuminating."

Tony began to speak. The sheriff held up a hand, realized what he was doing and then spoke to stall the words issuing from the jailbird's mouth.

"No, I'd rather you didn't really speak on your behalf. You'll be released today, as it pleases me. Then, you and your friend will get in your automobile and leave Queensburg. And we'll all be a lot happier.

"And for the record – those planes are just what I've told everybody else. Nothing. Nothing to get hung about. Army Air Force exercises. Mass hallucinations. Something that will blow over, Mr. Quinn."

Tony cooled his heels in the little cell for the rest of the morning and most of the afternoon. He listened – and covertly watched – as Sheriff Kent went about his duties and basically ignored his prisoner. Butch showed his face from time to time, hoping that his boss would be freed. Each time he was told to "come back later."

Throughout his incarceration, several things were observed by the young attorney. Hanging on the wall over his desk, the sheriff had a few framed documents and photos. The photos were of a youthful Kent in uniform, apparently about to head off for boot camp. The documents were, Tony guessed, the man's discharge papers and perhaps some sort of commendation. Despite Tony's amazing eyesight, the print was fine and the light bright on the white paper and no pertinent facts about the lawman could be determined absolutely. Nothing that would stand up in a court of law, he mused.

At approximately fifteen minutes after twelve o'clock, Sheriff Kent also had a visitor.

A short, rotund and thoroughly balding man of roughly the same age as the sheriff stuck his head in the door and Kent beckoned him to enter. Tony put on his very best blind-man's face and opened his ears as wide as they'd stretch.

The man was addressed as "Chester" by the sheriff, and Tony was able to glean that the man operated a radio station nearby. He also seemed to be somehow involved with a Queensburg volunteer fire brigade. He and the sheriff bantered back and forth a bit, but nothing too overly revealing to the lawyer. Then, with a sly look towards Tony, Chester motioned for Kent to remove himself to another room for further talk.

It all seemed innocent enough, thought Tony, but he had already learned – the hard way – that nothing was what it seemed in Queensburg along the Hudson River. After about ten minutes or so, the two men came out from the other room and Kent bid his visitor a goodbye. Tony caught a snatch of conversation referring to another person and "just get it done," but, again, nothing much more than those slender threads.

At five o'clock on the nose, Tony was told that he was being released.

"I'd like to issue a friendly warning to you and your friend, Mr. Quinn," said Sheriff Kent as he watched the blind attorney rub his wrists from the bite of the handcuffs. "Leave Queensburg. Now. And do not come back."

Tony smiled grimly. "Warning accepted, Sheriff. You won't see me again, I promise."

And it was a fact; Tony Quinn had no intention whatsoever of showing his face a second time in Queensburg. But he knew someone else who would be visiting in his stead. And soon.

"Nice town you got here, Sheriff," said Butch with a wink to the lawman as he opened the jailhouse door for Tony.

Kent slammed the door behind them.

"What do we do now?' asked the man-mountain, grumbling low in his chest.

"Back to the car," said his boss. "You fixed the tire, I assume? Good, then let's take our leave of Queensburg."

As they walked to the automobile, Butch could not help but inquire further as to Tony's plan. He itched to slug something. Or someone.

"Drive to the outskirts of town and find a nice, secluded spot," directed Tony. "But not on the highway. Find a dirt road somewhere. Somewhere within just a short walking distance of the downtown area."

Butch nodded, feeling more confident in discerning the lawyer's intentions. He drove off and within minutes found the type of spot Tony had described. He parked before a copse of shade trees, stalled the engine and fixed the brake. Turning around in his seat, he found his boss with a thoughtful expression on his roughly-handsome face.

Tony outlined his thoughts. "We know that someone is trying to scare the people of this town. There are a few suspects already, but there very well could be players we're not yet aware of. The sheriff is not only hiding something, but I can tell he himself is very concerned – he's scared, Butch. Almost as if, well, as if someone is holding something over his head. He's ex-military, most likely from the War, yet he carries a great weight upon his shoulders. I'd almost feel sorry for him if it wasn't that he may be covering up a scheme to sew panic among hundreds, maybe even thousands of people."

"Whew!" blew Butch. "What do we do about it? Where do we start? I'd like to get my little mitts on that Conklin, for one – and that teacher, now that I think of it! You think they were the mugs who jumped us in the alley?"

"No," said Tony, shaking his head. "That was Tulane and his pals; I could smell them. And 'we' are not doing anything here in Queensburg, Butch. Our friend the Black Bat is going to take a good, hard look at things – and *you* have matters to take care of in the city for me…"

At the mention of the Black Bat, the giant smiled. Though he was to be separated from his boss and sent away on a special mission, Butch knew the situation in Queensburg would be in very good hands, indeed. He listened carefully as Tony laid out directions for what he needed to accomplish in the city and then the two men sat back and waited for nightfall.

If anyone was present on that lonely stretch of road just outside the little town, and had waited around until dark, they might have spied a nondescript coupe sitting parked under some trees by the side of the road. They may have even spied or heard the rear door open and close. But the chances were slim that these imaginary voyeurs would have caught a glimpse of the strange personage that had exited the vehicle.

A tall, shadowy figure clad all in form-fitting black emerged. The man wore black, crepe-soled boots and black gloves that molded themselves to his long, supple fingers and tightly-muscled forearms. Across his shoulders hung an odd cape or cloak, which seemed to be a membranous thing, reminding one of sinister bat wings. Around his waist, a belt circled, presenting what appeared to be pouches for holding all manner of small tools.

Over the man's head and face an inky black cowl sat, hiding telltale scars. Naught but the eyes of the man could be seen underneath it. Those eyes glinted with purpose and determination. The man reached up to touch the stocks of the twin .45 caliber automatics which rested in holsters strapped to his chest. The eyes twirled with satisfaction.

The Black Bat nodded to the driver of the vehicle and with a swirl of the bat-like cape, the figure was gone. The car drove off, heading for the big city.

Silently clambering over the rooftops of the buildings of downtown Queensburg, the Black Bat's keen eyes scanned the urban terrain. Finally, he spotted his quarry across the street from where he had paused in his quest.

The man's eyes, which allowed him to see through darkness as an ordinary man sees in daylight, raked over the entirety of the police station. Satisfied that nothing seemed amiss, the Black Bat took in the rest of the surrounding buildings. Next to the station there appeared to sit a radio station. Atop its roof there were the usual smokestacks and piping, but also antenna arrangements and a few loudspeakers. There were lights burning in an upstairs room; the Black Bat assumed they were currently broadcasting. There was also a light on in the police station.

A few citizens walked the streets, on their way about their business. A short stroll down the street, the black-clad man could spy the Redcoat Diner, which was also apparently occupied. Nothing seemed too out-of-place; a nice, quiet little town.

The Black Bat wasn't all together sure what he was waiting for. What he hoped to see. There was something in the air, to be sure, but its properties were elusive – and foreboding. Something *would* happen, and he had only to wait patiently for it to occur.

While he waited, the Black Bat once again scanned the immediate area. After several visual passes, he noticed something. Each of the buildings in his immediate area sported flat vents of some sort, high atop their facades and on several different sides. These vents were fronted by fine grillwork. The Black Bat pondered this. After a moment's thought, he could discern no real reason behind such a design, unless they were a new sort of drainage system of which he was unaware.

A noise on the street brought him out of his reverie. He tensed and peered down at the sidewalks, sure in his concealment. There, exiting the police station and locking the door, was Sheriff Kent. The man looked around him, but not in a suspect manner, and took a step or two down the street.

Then, came the sound of planes.

The Black Bat froze, then listened. The droning sound of engines could be heard far in the distance, but then in an instant, the roar surrounded him. It was as if an entire squadron of fighter planes was directly overhead. He could practically feel their weight in the sky, but, as much as he tried, could not see the craft.

Down on the sidewalk, the sheriff started and leapt into action. The Black Bat saw the man bolt down the street and up to a few citizens who were caught by surprise by the sound. He enfolded them in his arms and pushed them towards a waiting doorway. They appeared startled and not a little amount frightened.

Then, the lights went out. The Black Bat looked all around, peering through the darkness, hoping for an answer to the queer occurrence to present itself. He was only further stymied; no solution appeared.

Suddenly, the sound of a nightmare approaching came to his keen ears. The unmistakable and terrifying tone of a bomb being dropped from an airplane filled the night air.

The Black Bat froze again, tensed all his muscles, opened up all his senses. He head swiveled around and around, vainly seeking the source of the horrible sound.

The world, the entire universe exploded around him. First, a deafening roar ripped at his ears. Then, a cataclysm of light and fire whipped at him. Finally, the roof below his feet buckled and caved. Every point on his body screamed as the building on which he stood seemed to disintegrate.

The Black Bat fell, and every bit of sanity and structure around him.

As everything crumbled around him in heat and fire, the Black Bat pitched himself forward as he began to fall. The movement was instinctual. The desire to survive overrode every other thought, every other compulsion. He knew neither where he was going nor what was ahead of him, but the Black Bat knew he wanted to live.

The sound of the explosion was deafening. The force of its detonation whipped at him, tore at his clothes. It also served to drive him away from its epicenter.

Leaping from the roof's edge, the Black Bat attempted to set his entire body into the pose of a cliff diver, those amazing fellows who purposefully plummet from great, craggy heights into frigid, choppy waters below. Beyond that, there was little conscious thought.

His hands and arms tautly in front of him, the Black Bat seemed a dark dart thrown into the void. His fingers connected with something and he grasped at it, desperate and amazed. It was a wire.

The dark-clad man held onto the wire for dear life. The material of the gloves he wore aided in his attachment to the wire. He prayed it would be thick enough to hold him.

Somehow, the wire was connected to a building or a pole on the other side of the street. Later, the Black Bat would realize that it might have carried electricity or telephone service to the building he'd been standing on. Now, it carried life – and escape.

It was over in a wink of an eye. The sound of the bomb dropping. The fiery cataclysm of the explosion. The building crumbling. The leap, the wire. Then, impact. Bone-crunching impact.

The Black Bat connected with what he presumed to be the façade of the neighboring building with a sickening thud. Every bone in his body – and he was in the most incredible condition a human being could aspire to – screamed in agony under the impact.

Still clutching the wire, he hung there, a crumpled child's toy. Across from him, the blaze of the bombed building lit up the night in colors of the Apocalypse.

Dazed and confused, the Black Bat opened his eyes to survey the scene. Rubble blazed bright as tall flames reached up into the night. He could hear many people yelling. There came the clanging of a single, strident bell, then many bells. He closed his eyes again, trying to assess his own condition. What had he witnessed? The bombing of a building in a small, New York town by enemy aircraft? How could this be possible?

The Black Bat realized he was adrift in the conundrum. He had nothing to anchor himself within its myriad facets. As he hung there, a dark shape illuminated by the bonfire, he thought of his friends, his loved ones, and their safety. If war had come to the shores of his beloved country, life as

"...the Black Bat's keen eyes scanned the urban terrain."

they knew it would be irrevocably altered.

Shaking himself out of his reverie, he focused on a decision: up or down. The Black Bat knew he could not continue to hang there, for all to see; he must ascend or descend, and quickly.

Though it would take every last iota of his vanishing strength, he decided to pull himself up to the roof above him. Once more he prayed, and this time with a specific focus on the stability of the wire from which he hung. Hand over hand, the Black Bat pulled himself up and to a better vantage point.

Once on the roof, he watched the scene across the street. He could barely hear, so loud was the detonation and so close he was to it.

Citizens of Queensburg ran to and fro, some in confusion, some with purpose. A volunteer fire brigade had organized itself and they now struggled with their hoses. The Black Bat also noticed a small crowd of people that began to form on the sidewalk across from the blaze. At the forefront of the grouping, he recognized a prominent figure.

It was Severn Drovik, the teacher. The Black Bat strained to make out what the frantic man was yelling about.

"...right here in Queensburg!" he heard the man screech. "Our little town, under attack! And for what? Why? Why? It's the war-mongers, I tell you! It's the men who crave war in Washington who've brought this down upon our heads! The people! The poor, poor people – we are the ones who must suffer for the...the...*greed* of the war-mongers!"

Amazingly, a few citizens around him shook their heads in agreement. One man even went so far as to clamp a hand on Drovik's shoulder in some sort of solidarity.

Suddenly, the round face of Frank Conklin appeared out of the crowd. Puffy-eyed and angry, he drove himself directly at Drovik, his hands balled into fists.

"You stupid *ass!*" the man screamed. "We've just...just been *bombed* and you stand there *pontificating*? People might be inside there," he gestured towards the blaze. "We've got to help them!"

The Black Bat then saw a woman behind Conklin grab the man's arm and push her face towards his. "No, no! It was empty! Don't you remember? It was vacated just two days ago!"

Here was another piece of the puzzle, the Black Bat figured. The building that was bombed was empty of people and perhaps all other valuables.

Coincidence? If so, it was a remarkable one.

He looked over at the fiery inferno to see that the hoses were now deployed and streams of water pumped out to fight back the immense tongues of fire. It was then that he spied Sheriff Kent and the man called Chester, the radio station operator and supposed fire chief of Queensburg.

The two stood calmly off to one side of the conflagration, apparently chatting with each other as if they were attending a small bonfire at a Halloween party.

The Black Bat's hackles rose at the sight. Then, he noticed the sheriff's attention seized by something across the street. Leaning over the side of the roof, he peered down to glimpse what it was that Kent now stared at.

It was Stanwald, the mute man from the diner.

The man just stood there, serenely, and looked around himself at all aspects of the scene. He watched as the teacher and the businessman argued, as the other people in the crowd seemed to choose a side either with their proximity towards the two combatants or simply with their eyes. He watched the people who fought the fire. He watched everything. Except for the sheriff.

What this meant, the Black Bat could not guess. Not at the moment. Every fiber of his being called out for him to help with the emergency, but he was transfixed by the dynamics between the crowd, the fire, the sheriff and Mr. Stanwald. Something was most definitely rotten in Queensburg.

Suddenly, the crowd parted and dark figures cut through it and to its head. The hooded men. The same who had attacked Tony Quinn and Butch O'Leary in the alley just the night before, yet now with more many more hands on deck.

The hooded men broke through and rounded on the people. The Black Bat could see they wielded clubs and other types of cudgels and blunt instruments. The men squared their shoulders and the leader raised both his arms.

"Go back to your homes!" he bellowed. "You shouldn't be out on the streets! It's too dangerous!" A few of the other hooded men snickered at that last comment.

Severn Drovik's face went livid. "Fascists!" he screamed. "We have every right to be out here! The town belongs to everyone – you can't tell us what to do!"

Incredibly, Frank Conklin slid over to Drovik's side and set his shoulder against the wiry teacher's own. "What the hell's the meaning of this? Who are you? What business is it of yours to tell us what to do?"

With no reply and with a simple flick of his wrist, the hooded leader advanced on the two men. His cowled compatriots followed. Chaos ensued as the goons began swinging and citizens began falling.

The Black Bat did not hesitate, though his every muscle protested this immediate swing into action. Grabbing the wire with which he had ascended to his perch, he rappelled back down the building and to the street below. At roughly fifteen feet above the pavement, he pushed off from the building's façade with his legs and let go the wire. Both citizens and goons looked up to see what appeared to be a demon straight from Hell flying towards them, its membranous bat wings spread out around it and its eyes blazing.

Landing just short of the mob, the Black Bat reached for the twin holsters strapped to his chest, with a mind to present a superior force compared to the clubs the goons carried. With a crushing surprise, he learned an awful truth: one automatic was missing. So muddled by the explosion and his harried escape from it was the avenger that he realized too late his negligence in checking his armament.

The momentary hesitation allowed the leader of the hooded men to re-gather his senses. He raised his cudgel and screamed. "Get him!"

The hooded mob descended on the Black Bat.

The hero ducked his head and, not waiting for the blows of the clubs, waded into his opponents. He lashed out with both fists. He sent vicious kicks left and right. His gloved hands and booted feet made stomach-turning impact on the bodies of the men, sending them helter-skelter backwards and sideways. Some grunted in pain. Other bellowed.

The Black Bat swung his cape into the face of one man and, once staggered, he opened himself up to a flurry of blows from the hero. As the man fell to the ground, the Black Bat once again caught the odor he had detected the previous day in the Redcoat Diner. With a flash of insight, he realized what it was: cordite. The smell of the explosive mixture was almost subtle, but strong enough to be identified.

He cursed himself for not placing it earlier. Another puzzle piece slid into place.

A savage blow to a spot between his neck and left shoulder told the Black Bat that it was no time for reverie. He wheeled around to stare into the face of a man who wore no hood. It was one of the townspeople.

The Black Bat defended himself. He could not bring himself to strike out at the man. He detected confusion, fright and not a small bit of panic. Ultimately, he was forced to lay the man low with a single, tight jab to the jaw.

The entire street broke out into unsecured chaos. The crowd surged in all directions and screaming and yelling droned out the sounds of the massive blaze from the bombed building. The Black Bat tried to take a few steps back and assess the situation.

He saw the hooded men fighting with the citizens. The citizens were holding their own; but many of them fell to wicked turns of the men's clubs.

It was then that the Black Bat turned to see Sheriff Kent standing off to one side, doing nothing. He looked pale and drawn. No expression was affixed to his face. The man looked like one of the living dead. There was no sign of Chester.

The dark-clad avenger turned back to the mob to see if he could spot Drovik and Conklin. He could not catch sight of either of them, but admitted that they could be both lying prone in the street, trampled underneath the melee.

Someone had caused this chaos. No, not just the hooded men; they were a part of it, of course, but they were most likely directed by another. Or a group of others.

Someone was benefiting from all the confusion and pain and suffering. Someone was putting the town of Queensburg through Hell on purpose.

As if in answer to the Black Bat's burning questions, the hooded leader, the one who had observed all in the alley the night before, appeared like a phantom. The avenger spotted him moving between two nearby buildings, a shadowy wraith gliding along through what little darkness that was not dispelled by the blaze. Then, in a heartbeat, he was gone. As if he was never there.

And so was Sheriff Kent.

The Black Bat unholstered his remaining automatic and fired two shots into the air. The crowd hesitated, seemed to be shocked by the sound. Faces turned from their fighting to look around blankly at each other.

The Black Bat aimed his sidearm at one of the hooded men and set his sights squarely between the man's eyes. Those eyes grew wide. Then, the man bolted. His fellows joined him.

Not waiting to gauge the further reaction of the townspeople, he turned and sprinted towards the spot in which that the hooded leader was last seen.

Finding himself in another darkened alley, the Black Bat, his automatic held before him and all his senses opened wide, dove into the inky shadows. To his heightened vision, it was as if the light from the blazing building had found its way to illuminate the area. He saw footprints in the dirt and followed them.

In actuality, it was two sets of footprints.

They led to a large grating on the side of one of the buildings, about thirty feet down the alley and at a dead-end. The grating sat at ground-level. The Black Bat could see where someone had gripped it in two different spots and in doing so, rubbed off some of the ancient grime that adorned it. Re-holstering his sidearm, he placed his own hands on the areas and pulled. The grating swung up, leaving an opening large enough for a man to stoop over and enter.

The Black Bat collected all his faculties and smoothed over his jangled nerves. Steeling himself for whatever may come, he slid into the opening and shut the grating behind him. Before him was a small room made of stone. Across the room was a smallish wooden door of antique vintage.

He stepped up to the door and, once determining that there was no trick to opening it, grasped its handle and swung it wide. He was a bit surprised at what he found behind it.

Tunnels.

The Black Bat looked out into what could only be described as a warren of underground tunnels. Stemming from a strange, octagonal central room, the tunnels branched out in every direction. They appeared to be of a very, very old construction.

He was then reminded of what the sheriff had told him; about Queensburg dating back to before the American Revolution and that British soldiers had attempted to burn the town down. Evidently, they had reason to believe the area was a hub of turncoats and rebels; perhaps these tunnels were where they originally lurked.

Stepping over lightly to the first doorway on his right, the Black Bat began to look for signs that someone had recently passed through. He had to find the hooded man, for he believed the answers to the puzzle of Queensburg lay with the mysterious personage. Having command of the tunnels would surely mean having command of the town, if what he suspected – that they honeycombed their way beneath the entirety of Queensburg – was true.

As he stooped to peer at the floor before the third doorway for signs of his prey, the Black Bat heard voices off in the distance. Someone far down the passageway was raising their voice. He could also faintly make out another voice answering.

The Black Bat hurried down the tunnel, his membranous cape flaring out against the damp, rough-hewn stone walls and ancient oak support beams.

After many twist and turns, he saw light ahead of him, dim yet promising. Then, again, voices. He hurried towards them. As he did so, he marveled at the amazing construction of the tunnels and the ingenuity of his country's forbearers.

The Black Bat stopped short of a room from which the light emanated. It appeared to be a sort of guard room or outpost. At the moment, there was little he could do to guess exactly what part of the town he was currently under. The voices rose again and he crept closer to listen.

"...*astounding* that here before me stands the vaunted 'Butcher of Alsace.' Who would have imagined that such a luminary would be so squeamish over such a minor action?"

The voice that spoke carried a coarse, guttural European accent. Its owner spoke slowly, deliberately, yet with power underlying the words. The Black Bat had not heard this voice before.

"I'm a changed man now," came the reply, barely a croak. "And you've taken this thing too far." It was the sheriff, the Black Bat realized.

'What would they say?" asked the other. "What if they possessed the knowledge that such an infamous character stood in their midst? No, friend Mahkent, you wouldn't want that, would you? That would be, I'm quite sure, a life-altering experience..."

"I want out," said the sheriff with something akin to assuredness. "Someone from the outside has finally tumbled onto what you're doing here. That blind lawyer from the city, and now...now this...this man in black."

Mahkent? The Black Bat pondered that. Possibly the sheriff's real name. He sorted through his thoughts, trying to pull up bits and pieces of data from the Great War, but an explosion of fury from the other figure in the room interrupted him.

"He will be dealt with!" bellowed the coarse voice. "As we did in the War! My experiment here is reaching a fever pitch and we stand on the threshold of a new stage in—"

The man's voice cut off. The Black Bat reasoned that he had to take the chance of exposure to be able to move closer and view the scene before him. He peered carefully around the frame of the door that led into the room, closer to the floor, so as to take a position that might be at first overlooked.

He saw Kent – or Mahkent – holding a pistol on the other man. That other was dressed head to toe in black robes, and sporting an inky black hood that covered his entire head and face, save his eyes. For the first time, the Black Bat noticed a symbol on the man's left breast – a stylized eagle in gold.

"I said I want *out*," urged the sheriff. "The people of Queensburg, they don't deserve this. *No one* would deserve this. I've got to find that man in black, that crusader, and…"

The Black Bat stood and straightened, then stepped into the light.

"Here I am."

Even bedraggled, burned and exhausted, the Black Bat cut an imposing figure. Both the hooded leader and the sheriff turned to look in unbridled astonishment at him.

A pistol appeared in the hand of the hooded man, a wicked-looking Luger. He began shooting.

Bullets tore at the stone and wood around the Black Bat, sending sharp splinters like tiny darts flying through the space he occupied. The sound was deafening in the little room, adding further pain to his already-addled ears. He flung himself backwards, seeking cover.

The hooded man screeched in his glottal language. Other men appeared, some dressed in hoods, others attempting to pull on their own. Their leader commanded them towards the intruder, to bring him back dead or alive.

The Black Bat dove back down the tunnels, knowing full well he was outnumbered and at a distinct disadvantage in the cramped, labyrinthian surroundings. He could see very well in the dark, but the space was too short and tight for suitable tactics and he was a stranger to the layout. Better to retreat. Besides, he had a new mission in mind.

Guns materialized in the hands of the mob of men and blazing shots rang out in the damp air of the tunnels like explosions. The flashes from the muzzles and the booming belches of the bullets served to disorient the Black Bat, but he pushed forward, holding onto what he believed was a picture of the way he had come in.

He came to a split in the tunnels and momentarily drew a blank on his directions.

Reaching for his remaining automatic he drew it and turned to fire behind him. Two of his pursuers grunted and dropped. A third fellow tripped over the prone body of one of the two and went sprawling. The Black Bat clubbed him savagely in the back of the head with the butt of his sidearm.

Then, he chose a tunnel and ran. Gunshots nipped at his heels, urging him ever forward.

The entire situation had reached a distinct point, he thought to himself. The hooded man was correct in that. The town of Queensburg was being waylaid by an insidious mind, but for what exact purpose he wasn't absolutely sure, though glimmers of it were coalescing in his brain. If only he could stop and think. Unfortunately, his pursuers weren't keen on allowing him that option.

Suddenly, he felt a breeze on his face and saw stars.

The stars were those in the sky and the breeze came through a grating set high in a wall of the tunnel he ran through. It wasn't the aperture through which he originally entered the maze, but it might just suffice to allow him to exit it. Across from the grating, on the opposite wall, was a wooden door.

The Black Bat listened for the gang that was tracking him. Then, he threw open the door, glad that it was not locked. Assessing the door's rusted hinges, he then kicked out violently with one booted foot, aiming to break one hinge. It shattered upon impact. The second hinge proved to be a bit more resilient, but it too broke under pressure and wrenching, and within seconds the Black Bat had the door loose.

He picked up the heavy oaken panel and, turning it somewhat sideways and diagonally, began to wedge it into place a short distance down the tunnel and past the grating. Satisfied at his work, the hero dove at the grating and attempted to pull it loose.

Then, his pursuers arrived.

The mob of goons hit the spot where the Black Bat had wedged the heavy wooden door and drew up short, surprised and confused. A grim smile crossed the avenger's face; the action had its intended outcome. In front of him, the grating was almost free from its moorings.

The men punched at the door, kicked at it. It held. They screamed in frustration. The Black Bat scrambled through the opening he had made, clawing for the outside world.

Shots rang out again. Stone splintered around him. Pain erupted in one of his legs, blossoming like a fiery flower through his flesh. He heard the crash of the wooden door hitting the floor.

He pulled himself through and looked around. He was on a street he didn't recognize, but one devoid of other human beings. There was no time for sightseeing. The hero turned back to the opening he'd just pulled himself through and took aim with his automatic.

The Black Bat fired once, twice. His gun then clicked-clicked-clicked. Empty.

He ran. The body of the man he had just felled would serve to choke the opening long enough for the Black Bat to flit away into the night.

A perfect landmark led him on through the darkened streets: the glow from the bombed building. The Black Bat had a singular purpose, and he prayed it would be enough to turn the tide of terror that was seeping into the town.

Though his leg burned, he hobbled on. Perhaps the bullet had passed cleanly through it, he thought, or maybe it was still lodged in his flesh. He did not know, but it also did not matter; he had a mission.

Moving closer to the center of town, the Black Bat could hear the sound of the Hudson River nearby. That made him think of New York and of Carol Baldwin and of Silk and Butch. He hoped Butch had made it through.

He found the building he was searching for and, avoiding the people who swarmed about, either in panic or with purpose, began to ascend its staircase.

It was tough going. The Bat was quite certain he was losing a lot of blood. He grit his teeth and set his jaw and pulled his weakened frame up the stairs. He must reach the top or everything was lost.

And he had something to say.

Finally reaching the roof, the Black Bat lurched over to the side of the building that faced the street and the earlier destruction. Looking over the edge, he saw that the hoses still pumped water onto the blaze and that crowds of people still stood around. Good, he thought. Perfect.

He spied Severn Drovik and Frank Conklin among the crowd. He also spotted Sarah Tobin and her two children. They looked a fright. Danny and Samantha's eyes reflected horror and suffering, and Sarah appeared

"The Black Bat stepped into the light."

as if her world had crumbled all around her little family. Maybe it had, he thought. Queensburg was her life. And now…

The Black Bat called out to crowd below.

"People of Queensburg!" he yelled, to snatch their attentions. "Please, listen to me! You have been done a massive injustice! You are being manipulated in a scheme that defies comprehension…"

He could see their faces turn upwards and try to focus on him. They were confused and tired. It was a pitiful sight.

"This building was not bombed from above!" he continued. Murmurs broke out among the townspeople with that statement. "It was bombed, yes, but from below – from explosives set by men right here in this town. Not from enemy aircraft in the skies!

"There are no airplanes!"

The Black Bat suddenly leaped over to a structure on the roof of the building. He laced his fingers into one of the flat vents that he had seen earlier and had wondered at. Pulling with every last reserve of strength he possessed, he ripped the vent's cover from its place in the wall.

Behind it was a loudspeaker. He let out a long breath. He was right.

The Black Bat tore at the speaker and wrenched it out of the hole in the wall. He then threw it down to the street below. It crashed into the pavement. The people looked at it dully. Confusion, then growing comprehension played across some of their faces.

"You have been rats in a cage!" yelled the Black Bat. "Pulled to the left and to the right! Made to think and feel what someone – the mastermind behind this entire affair – *wanted* you to think and feel!

"You've been complacent too long. It's time you woke up."

The Black Bat's head exploded with light and sound. The heavy blow that fell upon his skull knocked the wind completely from him and he dropped to his knees onto the rough surface of the roof. Another blow put him fully prone.

Hands gripped his cape, pulled on it to lift his head. A savage kick landed on his temple. Another on his jaw. He heard a short titter of mirth.

Then, he was pulled up and away. He watched as the glow from the burning building coalesced into a single ball of light and then into oblivion.

He awoke to the smell of must and stone and mold. Without opening his eyes, the Black Bat reckoned that he had been returned to the ancient tunnels underneath Queensburg. He also smelled sweat and cordite and felt the bite of shackles around his wrists.

"Good," said a deep voice. "Our guest awakens, yes? Help him reach full consciousness, eh?"

A bucketful of brackish, foul water hit him full in the face, his mask repelling most of the moisture. The Black Bat tasted some of the horrid liquid seeping through the black cloth onto his lips. He coughed and opened his eyes.

There before him stood the hooded man. Ringed around him were his lackeys. The Black Bat saw the bullet-headed Tulane and his partners staring at him intently. To one side stood Sheriff Kent, looking much worse for the wear and with apparently much of the fight taken out of him. His eyelids looked heavy and his mouth hung slightly open. Chester the fire chief covered him with a gun.

The hooded leader glanced from the Black Bat to Kent. "Allow me to introduce Martin Mahkent to you, my friend. Yes, you know him as 'Kent,' but I assure you that is an assumed name. He is much better known as Mahkent, the Butcher of Alsace."

The weird figure continued in his grumbling accent. "We knew each other on the battlefields of France, during the so-called 'Great War,' and as soldiers against your own country. Martin was a much more imposing figure in those days, yes, and, I should say, taught his enemies the meaning of fear. Did you know he slaughtered an entire town in the Alsace region, just as a delaying tactic for your troops, so that he might flee the battlefield?"

The Black Bat listened, but also began to assess his position. Heavy shackles and chains held him fast to a stone wall and he was surrounded by men with guns and clubs. It didn't strike him as particularly good position from which to assert himself.

Sheriff Kent groaned low in his throat. The hooded man chuckled.

"My former associate does not see eye-to-eye with me on his glorious past, no," he said. "But I remind him of it often. He tried to submerge it, you see, and came to America to make a new life, under a new name. But I remembered him and his deeds, and I told him, 'I will tell others, and they too will know you.' Mahkent didn't care much for that, but he saw my very good point.

"I myself have come to this country on behalf of my new leaders…or should I say my old leaders? Ah, that point is up for debate. But, regardless,

I have – how do you say? Set up shop? Yes, I have set up shop here and begun my experiments."

"Experiments?" queried the Black Bat.

"Yes," said the man quietly. "In terror."

A cold wave of air seemed to blanket the Black Bat. The hooded man's words chilled him. The weight of them, the meaning behind them, was outrageous. It took the wind out of the hero's sails.

"You see, my masked friend, my leaders would know of the current mettle of the American people. We are making great strides in terror overseas at this time, but what of the much-vaunted United States of America? How will its people react when our troops, our aircraft, make their approach to this land? And, mark my words, they *will* approach, and they *will* conquer. And my leaders would know in advance how your people feel, how they experience terror. So, my experiments, you see…"

"Insanity," said the Black Bat. Covertly, he tested his chains. By making it seem as if he strained a bit in excitement to get at his captor, he assessed their strength.

"Perhaps," said the hooded man, slowly, like a snake. "But insanity with a purpose. This town is very suitable for such an experiment, and with the good 'Sheriff Kent' aiding and abetting me, well, I must say – my tests are proceeding very nicely."

"The sounds of planes in the night," the Black Bat spit out. "Pressure and coercion from a mob of goons, even a building seemingly destroyed from a dropped bomb…"

"Yes, yes! You *do* see it! Your people are, surprisingly, easily led to feelings of fear! As we have increased the amount of terror, allowing it to build, I have observed this. My leaders will be very happy with this information."

The Black Bat shook his head. "And Kent has been covering for you." It was not a question. "He's been making sure no one leaves town, through cajoling—"

"And through force, if necessary," pronounced the hooded man. "Yes, Mahkent, though he protests, knows the value of such information. He knew its value on the rocky ground of Alsace, too."

"That was in *war*!" suddenly screamed the sheriff, his eyes now wide and his fingers clenching and unclenching.

"So, too, is this war, my friend," said the hooded man. Then, he shot Kent in the belly.

He watched as the man slumped to his knees and then fully to the stone floor, his dark, red blood oozing out of him and into the cracks between the stones.

This was bad, thought the Black Bat. As bad as he'd ever seen it. No sign of Butch, all alone and in chains, beaten and shot – not good at all. Perhaps he had failed. Perhaps he had bitten off more than he could chew there in Queensburg. But, he had only wanted to help people and in reward gotten a madman and his tests of terror instead.

"I see you have noticed my golden sigil here," said his captor, tapping the motif on his chest. "And you do not care for it. Yours is not the only country to use the eagle as a symbol, my friend. Only Americans would be so full of themselves to think they and they alone owned the right to bear such a proud creature.

"Now, I must tell you that you have done me an actual favor, yes. You have roused me from my experiments to show me, quite clearly, that it is time to move on. My work here, for the most part, is done. I have other, ah, 'irons in the fire' that I must check on, and I've grown tired of all of Queensburg's capitalists and smelly communists…and even the pretty diner owners…"

The hooded man looked over at Tulane then. He pointed at the Black Bat. "Unmask him and then kill him."

From somewhere down one of the tunnels came the sound of shouting. Then, the sound of shooting.

Tulane stumbled as he approached the Black Bat. He looked up, confusion on his face. Then, he glanced back at his master.

"Don't just stand there, you oaf!" screeched the hooded man. "Take some of your men and see—"

He never finished the statement. That was when the roof caved in, figuratively, though the Black Bat would have almost sworn it was literally.

The room was in a blink of an eye filled with yelling, screaming people brandishing a wide variety of weapons, some of them of the impromptu sort. Shots rang out. Men screamed. The Black Bat heaved and pulled at his chains.

One of the chains came loose from the old, rotting mortar which held it affixed to the wall. He looked up then to see Frank Conklin standing over him.

"We're here to rescue you!" yelped the businessman. "All of us! You woke us up!"

The Black Bat saw several townsmen he recognized, including Severn Drovik, the teacher. The gangly man was hefting a pitchfork, swinging it at one of the goons and yelling something about workers uniting.

Conklin helped the Black Bat pull the other chain from the wall. Then, all hell broke loose. The room was on fire.

Smoke filled the space rapidly. Men howled and pushed toward the exit. Frank Conklin's hand shot out to the black-clad hero, to help him to his feet. Then, they got out of there.

The hooded man was nowhere to be seen.

As the Black Bat and the men of Queensburg neared the outside world, a grumbling came from far behind them. Explosions. The cordite, thought the Black Bat. Whatever of it the goons were working with, some of it was still in the tunnels.

They picked up the pace to reach the outside. His wounded leg ached.

As the men neared their goal, driven by the fire and the explosions, the Black Bat spied what appeared to be another exit, just short of the main one. He dived off towards it and made his way into the open air. Finding himself in yet another alleyway, he looked around and headed towards the glow from the street. It was then that he ran into the hooded man.

They were at the mouth of the alley when they saw each other. The Black Bat witnessed the townspeople gathered outside the secret entrance to the tunnels, waiting for their men to return. Anxious faces all watched as the first of the brave men made their way out. He also spotted Sarah Tobin among the crowd.

The Black Bat then pounced on his former captor.

The hooded man's hand shot out and slugged the hero savagely in the jaw. In his hand was his pistol. The Black Bat was staggered, but kept his upright position. His own gloved hands shot out and grabbed his opponent, then planted a nasty blow of his own on the man's jaw.

"You've lost," said the Black Bat through gritted teeth. "The citizens of Queensburg have thrown off the yoke of your 'experiment.' There's no terror here, not now."

Thrown up against a wall, the hooded leader rubbed his jaw through his mask. He cackled a bit.

"No terror, eh?" he said, low and menacing now. "I beg to differ."

His cruel-looking pistol appeared once more, seemingly from nowhere. He pointed it into the crowd. The Black Bat saw the man's target: Danny and Samantha Tobin.

"*Here is terror!*" screamed the hooded man.

Often times, those events that come upon us swiftly and by surprise do so in slow-motion. So it was when one of the most evil men the Black Bat had ever encountered drew a bead on two innocent children with a pistol and began to squeeze its trigger. The world crawled to an almost-standstill.

The Black Bat saw the hammer of the Luger move backwards, saw the soldier-like stance of triumph of the hooded man. He also saw Sarah Tobin's realization of the situation. He saw her terror. She dove in front of her children in slow-motion, a mother bear protecting her cubs, anger and disbelief written across her face. But also a fierce defiance.

The hammer started to come down and the Black Bat stretched through the quicksand of time to prevent a bullet from exiting its chamber and ending a life.

Then, he saw the muzzle of the Luger pointing at himself. There was a searing, blinding flash, then a loud boom. He felt his fist connect with the hooded man, saw his head lurch back, as if on a spring, and his entire cloaked form crumble and shatter.

Time speeded up again and clicked back into place.

The Black Bat, though, was blind.

He somehow made it away from the area without anybody seeing him leave. Behind him, as he moved hurriedly down an alley, his fingers staying in contact with the brick wall to guide him along, he heard someone yelling.

"It was Mr. Stanwald!" came the voice. The Black Bat nodded to himself. The "mute" man who could not disguise his accent, not like Mahkent could.

Then, he heard sirens. That would be Butch O'Leary and the State Police, he mused.

"So it was all a big flummox?" asked Butch. He turned to look at Tony Quinn, who lounged in the back seat of the automobile. His boss had seen much better days, and looked it.

"The airplanes, yes," replied the attorney. "But not the fear. That was, unfortunately, very real. The people of Queensburg were led into a grip of fear by a man who used them like…like guinea pigs. Tragic."

"And this Stanwald?"

Tony sighed. Even that made him hurt. "You heard Frank Conklin yourself, Butch – in the confusion and chaos, the man spirited himself away. But, at least his manipulation of this town is over. The cost was high, but I think these people have learned something about themselves and, maybe, even how to relate to each other.

"What bothers me right now is something Stanwald said, about having other experiments going."

"You mean to say that this same thing could be going on in some other town?" asked Butch. "It's incredible! Here in America!"

"It can happen anywhere, Butch," said Tony. "Stanwald had the help of an experienced soldier, someone who knew how to grapple with men's minds. Sheriff Kent was an unwilling partner in this 'test of terror,' but nonetheless, he aided in its deployment. Him and some home-grown sympathizers for a certain European country…"

The man-mountain clenched his fists. "Boy, would I like to get my mitts on them!"

Tony sat up in his seat. He looked over the rims of his dark glasses at the little town. Smoke still drifted upwards from a few spots. His sight was returning. His good humor was not.

"You may get your chance yet, pal," he said, patting the big man on the shoulder. "We need to stay vigilant and keep an eye and an ear out for trouble that smells of that rat and his followers. America's going to need every one of its citizens hale and hearty and wide awake for the harrowing days ahead…"

Butch O'Leary smiled grimly, nodded, then turned and put the motorcar in gear. They pulled away, leaving little Queensburg, New York behind.

The End

THOUGHTS ON THE BLACK BAT

Writing the Black Bat is the next best thing to writing Batman. Okay, I said it, so let's just move along, eh? Nothing to see here...

In all seriousness, the Black Bat is one of the pulp heroes I wanted to write most when I first started writing pulp. I'm pleased and honored to finally be afforded the unique opportunity to work with the character. I love Batman, sure, but at this stage in the game I think my chances of crafting an official Batman story are pretty low. I also love the original Dr. Mid-Nite comic book character, another "blind man," but, well, let's just say that the Black Bat provides me with the chance to write both Batman *and* Mid-Nite, all in one neat package.

Tony Quinn, to my mind, is a hero who's overcome adversity to throw a few punches at evil. He becomes most interesting, to me as a writer, when he plays at being blind, all the while gathering information and making his plans for an outing as his costumed alter-ego. As the Black Bat, he's very cool, of course, but as Tony he's got to juggle several things in the role. At any moment he could fumble the ball and send both his careers straight down the tubes. How he manages it all is beyond me.

"The Terror Test" went through several permutations before I sat down to write it, maybe more than any other story I've created to date. The core idea, of planes in the night frightening people, was there from the start, but the location and the reasons behind it changed as I laid out the plot. Originally, the story was set in the Black Bat's hometown of New York City, but the thought of taking him out of his comfortable setting and tossing him to the wolves in a place that was strange to him soon became too interesting for me to deny. So, Queensburg, New York, was born... along with its problems.

The town allowed me significant play with the idea of enemy planes bothering its citizens, more than I could achieve with a sprawling metropolis like New York. It also was a place that I could populate with my own sheriff and all the other people you've already met there. Besides, I think our villain would have had a much, much more difficult time trying to convince New Yorkers that they were being visited by enemy aircraft at night.

I hope you enjoyed my villain and his scheme, by the way. You may have noticed that he wasn't really brought to justice; that means I'd love to bring him back for a rematch with Tony Quinn some day…or some other pulp hero! And before I forget, other than "Stanwald" he has an Official Villain Name, too, though there wasn't enough time to tag him with it in the story. For the record, he's the "Black Eagle." Ooh, scary!

All his goons were brought to justice, though, just in case you were wondering.

Finally, as is my tradition in these author essays, here are the chapter titles for the story, in order: "For the Want of a Tire Iron," "Terror Above," "The Black Bat Takes Wing," "Explosions," "Terror Below" and "Tight Fit for a Bat."

Thanks, as always, for reading. Let me know what you thought.

JIM BEARD, a native Toledoan, was introduced to comic books at an early age by his father, who passed on to him a love for the medium and the pulp characters who preceded it. After decades of reading, collecting and dissecting comics, Jim became a published writer when he sold a story to DC Comics in 2002. Since that time he's written Star Wars and Ghostbusters comic stories and contributed articles and essays to several volumes of comic book history. Recently, he edited a book of essays on the 1966 Batman TV series, GOTHAM CITY 14 MILES.

Currently, Jim provides regular content for Marvel.com, the official Marvel Comics website, is a regular columnist for Toledo Free Press and is also writing a book about the comics industry during the decade that made him the huge fan he is today, the 1970s.

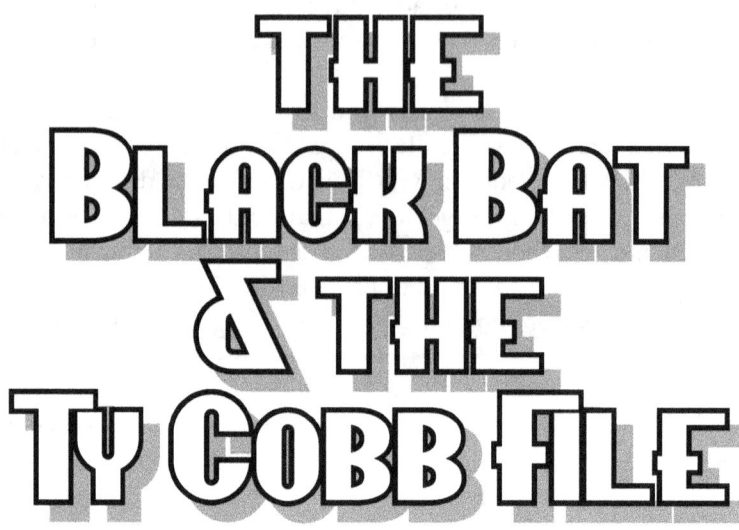

A Black Bat Adventure

by
Freank Byrns

Even as the hands wrapped around his ankles squeezed tighter and tighter, Sticky Fitzpatrick could think only of Scooter.

He barked a short, deranged laugh at the absurdity of it all. It was crazy to think that a man being dangled out of a twelfth-story office window by his ankles could think of nothing but whether or not he had fed his dog at home before he left for the night. Yet that's exactly what he was doing.

"One more time," the black gloves around his ankles growled. Well, not the gloves exactly. More like the man wearing the gloves, but from Fitzpatrick's disadvantaged viewpoint, those dark gauntlets were all that he could see.

"Last chance," the gloves continued. "Who are you working for?"

Fitzpatrick was working for Willie Rothschild, but he had every intention of keeping that fact to himself. When Rothschild had hired him for this job, it had seemed pretty simple, pretty straightforward. A late-night break-in at some fancypants lawyer's uptown office, your basic smash n' grab. And Rothschild wasn't looking for cash, jewels – nothing like that. "Anything like that you come across in the course of the job, you keep for yourself," the East Side crime boss had said. "Less my twenty percent, of course."

No, all Rothschild was after was some files. Second file cabinet from the right, third drawer down from the top. In and out in less than five minutes. Easy.

Or it should have been.

Fitzpatrick shook his head, banishing the image of a starving Scooter to the corner of his mind. He had to think fast, not an easy task for him under ideal circumstances. A pigeon flew past, close enough that FItzpatrick's hair was lifted in the breeze generated by the bird's wings. Not an ideal situation at all.

If he so much as mentioned Rothschild's name, he'd be taking a quick trip to the bottom of the Hudson River by the end of the week. He was sure of it. He'd seen it happen. But on the other hand... If those black gloves wrapped around his ankles belonged to the man he *thought* they belonged to...

The right glove squeezed tighter around Fitzpatrick's boot; the round bone in his ankle gave slightly with a muffled *crack*. He bit back a scream.

"Nothing to say?" the gloves said.

Fitzpatrick hadn't seen his attacker at all. His back had been to the door, jimmying the file cabinet open. Next thing he knew – literally one *breath* later – he had been wrapped up by a pair of powerful black-clad arms, lifted off his feet, flipped upside down, and dangled out the open window. The very window he had popped open just two minutes prior.

"Okay, then," the gloves said, just before letting go of his feet.

The scream died in Fitzpatrick's mouth before the first syllable was even heard – then picked right up where he left off as the gloves grabbed his ankles once again. He hadn't fallen very far – two inches, maybe three – before the impossibly-powerful hands grabbed his ankles once again. The impact of the sudden stop nearly pulled his legs out of their sockets. He had a sickly suspicion that this wasn't the first time the gloves had run this play. "Oops," the gloves said gruffly.

"Rothschild," Fitzpatrick said, the words leaking out of his mouth before he even realized they were doing so. The words flowed slowly, keeping pace with the tears leaking from his eyes and the damp stain spreading across his lap. "I'm working for Willie Rothschild."

"Hmm." The gloves lifted Fitzpatrick slowly, up above the window sill and back into the office. Then up further still, until their owner stood, arms high above his head, Fitzpatrick's feet still firmly in his grasp. Fitzpatrick's suspicions were confirmed: the black gloves belonged to a man dressed head to toe in black, a dark cape and mask to match. Twin .45's were nestled in the black belt slung around his waist, joined there by a wide assortment of tools and other unimaginable implements.

Though Fitzpatrick had never seen the man in the flesh before – few had, not that they lived to tell about it – he knew exactly who it was. The stories whispered in seedy underground gatherings were legendary; the legends spread in prison cells around the city were terrifying.

The black gloves belonged to The Black Bat.

Even at thirty-seven, Carl Hubbell could still buckle knees. True, his legendary screwball had lost a little something since that magical day in '34 when he struck out a veritable Who's Who of the American League –

Ruth, Gehrig, Foxx, Simmons, Cronin. *In order.* – in front of a hometown
All-Star Game crowd hanging from the rafters of the cavernous Polo
Grounds.

But still.

There were days – days like today – when he found a little bit of that
old magic.

"The old boy's got it all working today, doesn't he?" Police Commissioner
Jerome Warner turned to his companions in the box seats behind home
plate, his question asked between bites of his second hot dog.

"I'd say so. He's popping that mitt like a man ten years his junior." New
York Mayor Fiorello La Guardia tossed back another handful of popcorn,
then whistled as Hubbell painted the outside corner with a fastball that
Dodger shortstop Pee Wee Reese took for a called third strike to end the
inning.

Seated between these two pillars of the Gotham community, former
District Attorney Tony Quinn smiled, the thin lines of the scarring around
both eyes barely visible behind the dark glasses he wore. He tapped his
cane on the stadium's concrete concourse, echoing the raucous crowd's
applause. "I always thought you more of a Yankees man, Mr. Mayor,"
Quinn said.

"Well," La Guardia said with a wink he knew Quinn could not see. "The
mayor of a city with three teams can ill-afford to have a favorite."

The mayor and commissioner both turned as the man seated directly
behind Quinn snorted, trying in vain to suppress a laugh. The pair fixed
him with a cold stare.

"You doing all right back there, Mr. Kirby?" Warner asked.

Silk Kirby smiled, dabbed at his forehead with an Egyptian cotton
handkerchief. Despite his relatively low station as Quinn's personal valet,
Kirby was easily the best-dressed of the foursome, resplendent as ever
in a dark gray suit complete with tiny, nearly-invisible white pinstripes.
"Sorry," Kirby said. "Having a little trouble swallowing."

Quinn turned around at this, and despite the glasses, Kirby had no
doubt his employer's stare matched that of the others. "What? My hot dog.
Had a little trouble swallowing that last bite."

Quinn turned back around without a word to Kirby. Kirby took
another bite of his hot dog. "You'll have to excuse Silk," Quinn said to the
mayor. "Good help is so hard to find these days." He tapped his cane on the
cement for extra emphasis. "But a necessary evil."

"You don't have to tell me about good help," La Guardia said. "You're sure we can't persuade you to come back down to City Hall? Things just haven't been the same in the D.A.'s office since you left."

Quinn shook his head. "I wish I could, Mr. Mayor. But given my. . . *condition*, I think I would just feel more comfortable here in private practice."

La Guardia reached over, patted Quinn on the hand, efforting sympathy. "Of course, son." The mayor withdrew his hand, changing subjects quickly. "Speaking of private practice – yours was not one of the offices hit in these recent break-ins, I hope?"

"No sir – not yet, at least."

"O'Leary still hanging around your place?"

"Sometimes."

"Good. If I were you, I'd see that that big galoot spent as much time as possible in your office." La Guardia looked past Quinn, fixing Commissioner Warner with a pointed stare. "At least until this whole thing blows over."

Warner loosed a barely audible sigh. "As I said in your briefing yesterday, sir, we're following up several leads on this one, exploring every possible angle."

Down on the field, the Giants' fading slugger Mel Ott lay two bats down in the on-deck circle, keeping a third in his meaty paws as he headed towards the plate.

La Guardia pointed down at the bats, with the subtlety of an entire herd of elephants in a china shop. "Have you considered. . . any *special* measures?" he asked Warner.

Warner sighed again, quite loudly this time. Kirby snorted again. "Every *possible* angle," Warner said, his words whistling through tightly clenched teeth.

"Much to Lieutenant McGrath's chagrin, I'm sure," Quinn said lightly.

"Yeah, well, sometimes the Lieutenant is too smart for his own good," Warner said. "I spend a good deal of time reminding him about staring down the throats of gift horses."

"Or gift *bats*," La Guardia said, punctuating his words with an exaggerated, knowing nod.

Behind them, Kirby snorted again.

Warner turned to Quinn, eager to shift the conversation. "I've got two tickets for tomorrow's doubleheader that I can't use – box seats, right behind the plate. Yours if you want them."

"Sunday afternoon at the ballpark," Quinn said. "Doesn't get much better than that – whaddya say, Silk? Free tomorrow?"

"No can do, Bossman – not tomorrow, anyway," Kirby said, leaning over to slap Quinn on the shoulder. "I gotta see a man about a horse."

Clearly, Silk Kirby was a frustrated man.

Sighing deeply, he slid his thumb up under the band of his hat. He massaged his temple as he jabbed at the racing form in his lap with the dull point of his yellow pencil stub. He circled Idiot's Delight in the first, then scratched through it just as quickly. Kirby had walked through the track's gate at 12:15; it had taken less than twenty minutes for the original newsprint of the tout sheet to be all but invisible beneath his own tortured scribbling.

"Shame they don't make one of these with an eraser," he said, to no one in particular.

"How's that?"

Kirby looked up from his form to his right, towards the other end of the wooden bench, where a rather dapper gentleman in a white linen suit was looking his way. The man tapped his ear, smiling. "Hearing's not what it used to be," he said.

Kirby nodded, then repeated himself. He held up the pencil nub for emphasis.

The man smiled again, then held up his own form, as much a disaster as Kirby's. "No argument here," he said.

Kirby slid to his right, moving down the bench towards the man to make room for another man, this one in a black suit and hat, his own racing form pristine, unmarred by gambler's lament. *He must have just gotten here*, Kirby thought. *Give him time. Post time's not until one.*

The older man had placed his hat on the bench beside him, a white straw number that matched his suit, a small blue feather tucked into the band. He picked it up to make room for Kirby, then spun it on his finger once before dropping it back on his head. "So who you liking in the first, young fella?"

"I don't know," Kirby said. "I was leaning towards Idiot's Delight, but then I got a look at him out in the paddock. You could count his ribs." Kirby motioned towards his new friend's form. "See anything you like?"

"I like Double Down in the first – his jockey's been on a hot streak all week."

Kirby looked down, made a small circle around the number, three horse in the first. "Twelve to one – you sure?"

The old man smiled. "Oh, I'm *always* sure. Rarely right, though."

"Hey, that's good enough for me. How about the second race?"

"Oh, let's see... Red Baron looks good. The seven."

"All the way from the outside, huh? I like your style, pal."

"Flattery will get you everywhere, my friend – I'll give you the third race for free. Take Fool For Love."

"Fool For Love, riding the rail all the way to the winner's circle," Kirby said, circling the number one. "You gonna be around later on? If even one of these tips hit, I owe you a drink."

The old man shook his head. "Nah, I got a dentist's appointment in an hour. Tell you what, though – drop by the Calico Club on Wilmont. You'll find me there more nights than not. You can pay me back there."

Kirby reached out, shook hands. The old man's steady grip belied his age. "That's a bet, pal."

Kirby shifted his weight, making to leave, but the old man kept a firm grasp on his hand. "Now hold on, young fella – you wouldn't take my three best tips and leave me with nothing of the kind, would ya?"

Kirby scanned his racing form one last time, stopping on the day's sixth race. He couldn't help himself. "Bats in the Belfrey in the sixth," he said, barely biting back a smile. "Exacta box him with Crime Doesn't Pay."

"371 Wilmont Avenue. You're sure?"

Kirby removed his hat, dropped it on the passenger side of the car's bench seat. He dabbed his handkerchief on his forehead, then turned over the ignition.

He took a look in the rearview mirror, glancing at Quinn in the back seat, his employer's eyes all but unreadable behind his dark glasses. "Positive," Kirby said. "He gave me the three horse in the first, the seven in the second, and the one in the third. And then a non-existent bar on Wilmont."

Kirby backed out of the parking space, then eased them into the steady stream of cars leaving the racetrack. "And you're sure it was the right guy," Quinn said.

"He had a blue feather in the band of his hat – that's his trademark." Kirby goosed the engine to make a light, turning right and heading towards the Quinn estate. "Plus, a G-Man straight out of central casting sat down on the bench beside me in the middle of our conversation. I saw two more of them hanging out by the bathroom with a clear line of sight on the man."

Kirby turned to look back over the bench, making eye contact with the dark glasses Quinn always wore in public. "I'm telling you, Boss," he said earnestly. "I just made a date with Willie Rothschild."

The kid in the ring had quick hands; if he'd had footwork to match, he could have been a real contender. As things stood, though, he was flat on his back, counting lights, the match suddenly, unmistakably, over.

The whole thing had left Butch O'Leary more than a little frustrated. O'Leary had spent the entire week – and most of the previous week, too – just *sitting*, perched on an understuffed high-backed chair just inside the door of Tony Quinn's downtown office, *waiting* for a robbery attempt that might never come.

If there was one thing O'Leary hated more than sitting, it was waiting; to have to do both, at the same time, for weeks on end? Pure torture.

He was glad to do it, of course; the loyalty O'Leary paid to Quinn bordered on fanatical. They had considered each other friends for a long while now, and there was nothing O'Leary wouldn't do for a real friend.

But still. O'Leary figured it was probably wrong that he spent most of Thursday and all of Friday praying that someone *would* try to break in, just so he could get off the chair and on his feet and let his famous fists fly.

So when O'Leary heard about this young up-and-coming fighter Paddy Malone, he knew where he'd spend his Sunday afternoon. The plan had been to head over to Sully's Gym and watch the Malone kid work out a few rounds and see if the rumors were true. But when Sully asked Butch to climb into the ring and spar a few rounds with the kid – "C'mon, Butchie, just for old times' sake, y'know, see what he's got" – the past few weeks' inactivity came rushing back all at once.

So there he was, standing in the corner with borrowed gloves that were laced a little too tight, wearing borrowed trunks that rode up in the crotch a little too high. There he was, standing over the groaning body of young Paddy Malone, another would-be contender left wondering what might have been.

"Christ, Butchie, did you have to hit him so *hard*?" Sully said. O'Leary knew Sullivan wasn't angry, not really; better to find out your fighter's a bum in the controlled conditions of your own gym than under the bright lights of a championship prizefight.

"I pulled the punch, Sully." O'Leary shrugged. "I thought the kid could let it slide off."

"I guess you thought wrong." Sully handed O'Leary a towel as the ex-fighter stepped through the ropes and down to the floor. Up in the ring, Malone rolled over slowly, mumbling to himself.

O'Leary followed his old friend to a small office partitioned off in the corner of the gym, walking past a couple of kids working heavy bags along the wall and another pair jumping rope. "Business pretty good?" he asked, as Sullivan dropped into a rickety wooden chair behind his desk.

O'Leary took a chair on the other side and began unwrapping the tape that covered his hands.

"Can't complain," Sully said. "Other than the fact that you just exposed my next meal ticket."

"I thought he would –"

"Forget it. I'm just busting your balls." Sully reached into a desk drawer, pulled out two thick cigars. He offered one to O'Leary, who declined.

"Suit yourself," Sully said, striking a match on the desktop. "So what's going on with you, big guy? Still picking up work from Quinn?"

"Last couple weeks, yeah."

Sully shook his head. "Never thought I'd see the day – Battlin' Butch O'Leary, punching the clock for some uptown lawyer. Bet the pay's pretty good, though."

O'Leary shrugged. "It could always be better – any hot tips for me?" He turned and looked through the open office door towards the ring, where Malone was just now getting to his feet. "Any *other* tips, I mean?"

"Har har." Sully took a deep drag on the cigar, then exhaled, filling the small room with acrid smoke. "Now that you mention it, I do keep hearing about something big coming up."

"Something big?"

"Yeah. Heard it from several different bookies – some connected, some not – something big's coming. Gonna be a lot of money to be made."

"Any idea what it is?"

"Not really. Everybody's talking about it, but nobody's *talking* about it, know what I mean?"

"Not really, no."

"Ask your pal Kirby – ol' Silk's got ears on the street. Probably knows more about it than I do."

"Some kind of fix or something, you think?"

"Gotta be. Rothschild's name keeps popping up. If The Butcher's *really* involved, my money's on a fix."

O'Leary was right, Quinn thought as he felt the would-be mugger's nose relocate beneath his black-gloved fist. *It feels good to get out of the office sometimes.*

It felt good to be out on the street. It felt good to lose the dark glasses and cane, the affectations of a man playacting at being blind. It felt good to put on the dark gloves. The cape. The cowl. The twin .45s.

In short, it felt good to be The Black Bat.

For most of New York, Anthony Quinn was a tragic story, the flashy young District Attorney blinded when a gang of vengeful criminals threw blinding acid into his face. For those Gothamites, the story ends with the once-handsome young man broken and scarred but not unbowed, returning to the courtroom from time to time as a special contractor for the D.A.'s office. Few knew the story's true second chapter, in which a small town policeman's resourceful and intelligent daughter arrived with a longshot procedure that seemed so far beyond the pale as to be pure fantasy; but, impossibly, it worked, and Quinn rose from the surgeon's table, his sight restored. And fewer still knew the current, ongoing chapter: Quinn's five senses supremely enhanced, his body in peak physical form, waging a one-man war on crime in the streets of New York, fighting the low-life criminals with their own weapons – treachery, intimidation, theft; making his own laws, enacting his own judgments, all while wearing the mask of The Black Bat.

A routine Sunday night patrol had led the Bat to this spot, a dark midtown alley that split two of Gotham's finest restaurants. The post-theater crowd was out in full, dressed to impress in evening finery. Two such young ladies had stopped at the mouth of the alley for a decidedly un-ladylike quick cigarette – and that's when their attacker struck.

And that's when The Black Bat struck.

The Bat's punch sent the low-life stumbling backwards, coming to rest on the seat of his pants against a garbage can along the alley's back wall. The mugger spit a mouthful of blood onto the ground, then reached inside his jacket.

"Don't be stupid," the Bat said – but it was too late. He caught a glimpse of metal as the man wrapped his hand around the grip of a small revolver. The man was fast – but the Bat was faster. He unholstered one of the .45s and put two bullets in the criminal's chest before the gun even cleared his waistband.

The Black Bat turned back to the two women, cowering in fear near the alley's entranceway. "I'm sorry you ladies had to see that," he growled. "You probably don't want to watch this, either." The women took the warning to heart, scrambling back out onto the sidewalk towards the restaurants. The Bat watched them leave; satisfied he had the alley to himself, he reached into his belt for a small blade.

Police sirens howled in the distance as the Bat knelt over the criminal's corpse. "I told you not to be stupid," he said to the body, knowing his gunshots had drawn the authorities. He knew he had to move quickly.

The Black Bat stood, admiring his handiwork – a bat-shaped scar carved into the forehead of another hapless thug. *Let's not leave McGrath and his friends any doubt who's responsible for this*, he thought. He turned and bounded up a fire escape to the roof of the building, watching from above as the sirens drew closer.

An earnest, fresh-faced beat cop jogging up the sidewalk was first on scene; the Bat watched with interest as the two girls gave him the quick rundown of the last few minutes. A pair of blaring patrol units pulled up next, followed in short order by an unmarked detective's car. The car door flew open violently and the bulky Lieutenant McGrath extricated himself from the passenger seat, moving into the alley with a full head of steam, barking orders at everyone as he did so just in case there was any question as to just who exactly was in charge here.

The Black Bat peeled back one of his long gauntlets to peek at the wristwatch stitched into the inseam. Nearly ten o'clock – he'd wasted enough time here. Time to get moving.

Silk Kirby dabbed at his forehead, using the back of the gloves Rothschild had insisted they wear to wipe the sweat from his brow. It had been a while since he last picked a lock – his rustiness was making him nervous. And the stupid gloves weren't helping.

"Hurry it up, will ya?" The young hood standing behind Kirby breathing down his neck wasn't helping, either. And neither was the triple onion

"…did you have to hit him so hard?"

chili dog the kid had been shoveling down his throat back at the meeting with Rothschild.

Kirby hated working with a partner. In his previous vocation of all-around ne'er-do-well, he had only worked with others when the grift required. And he never worked with one as obviously inexperienced as Jack or John or Jimmy or whatever this kid's name was.

"What's your name again, kid?" Kirby asked without turning around. He kept his eyes and fingers focused on the deadbolt at hand.

"Stevie."

Wow, that's not even close, Kirby thought. He gave his wrist a slight twist, felt the pin drop back into place. *Dammit.*

"See, here's the thing, Stevie," Kirby said, flexing his fingers, taking a breather. "I didn't ask you to come along. I don't need you here, and I don't want you here."

Kirby felt Stevie lean back. He pictured the kid bowing his shoulders, indignant. "Yeah?" Stevie said. "Mr. Rothschild wanted me here."

That much was true, Kirby knew.

"Never knew you were a second-story man, Kirby," Rothschild had said earlier in the evening, when Kirby had come calling at 371 Wilmont. The address turned out to be a poorly lit and even-more-poorly signed hole-in-the-wall delicatessen. Kirby walked past twice before he even noticed it.

Chairs sat upside down on every table as he entered, the floor freshly swept and mopped; the Sunday lunch crowd had long since departed for home. A hanging bell clanged softly as the door clicked shut behind Kirby. The front of the house and the deli counter were dark, the only light in the entire place provided by a bare bulb hanging from the ceiling in the kitchen in the back.

"Mr. Kirby," a voice called from the kitchen. "Quick as ever – glad you were able to crack the code, as it were." Willie Rothschild, the crime boss of the East Side, stepped into the light, the blood and raw meat on his hands matching the front of the red apron he wore over a white shirt and white linen pants. "You'll forgive me if I don't shake hands."

"Not a problem, sir," Kirby said. He pictured his own fine Italian suit covered in gore, then blinked hard to clear his mind of that image. "You, uh... you need some help back there?" he asked, hoping against hope that Rothschild needed no help at all. With *whatever* he was doing back there.

"I appreciate the offer, but I was just wrapping up," Rothschild said with a cold smile. "I like to come down here some nights, help make the sausage for the next day's breakfast crowd. Takes my mind off things –

very soothing."

Rothschild pointed a bloody-pink finger towards the counter, where a state-of-the-art steel Belken electric slicer sat. "Of course, we have the modern amenities – gets the kids excited. But sometimes I'm an old-fashioned guy, yeah?"

Kirby wasn't sure what to make of that, so he didn't even try. "Should we sit down?" he asked instead, gesturing to one of the tables near the door.

"In a minute," Rothschild said. "First, though, I have to ask: how'd you know to find me at the track this afternoon?"

Kirby was ready for this; for once, he could just tell the truth. "Ran into Sticky Fitzpatrick last week – he told me you might have a couple of jobs coming together. Said I should just bump into you at the track one Sunday, see what happened."

Rothschild nodded. "When was this?"

Kirby shook his head, frowning. "I don't know – Thursday, maybe? Wednesday? Being perfectly honest, between you and me? I was a little. . . *overserved* at the time, if you know what I mean."

"I do."

Kirby reached inside his jacket, pulling out his wallet. He made a show of rifling through the mess of papers inside: diner receipts, cocktail napkins, business cards, an occasional dollar bill. "I know I have his number in here somewhere – we can give him a ring at his mom's place. He'll vouch for me – we celled together upstate a while back."

Rothschild smiled again, impossible to read, even for an experienced con like Kirby. "That won't be necessary, Mr. Kirby. Your reputation preceeds you. I would, however, be interested in that phone number."

"Yeah, sure," Kirby said, still poking around. "You need to talk with Stick?"

"I do. Some unfinished business from Friday night left to discuss."

Kirby knew full well what business that was. "Here you go," he said, handing Rothschild a number he'd picked up off a steakhouse waitress a few weeks back. "I think this is the one. When you talk to him, let him know he still owes me that last round."

Rothschild moved a few steps to his right and removed a chair from the tabletop closest to him. He motioned for Kirby to do the same. "As I said, your reputation precedes you here," Rothschild said once both men were seated. "Never knew you were a second-story man."

Kirby was ready for this one, too. "So you know I've been working for

Tony Quinn lately," he said carefully, mixing just the right amount of apprehension into his voice.

"I do."

"So you can imagine I've been moving in some different circles these days. Hanging out with a higher caliber of scoundrel."

Rothschild gave a smile at this, one Kirby read as genuine. "I can imagine."

"So you see all these guys, with all their *things*. . . hard not to want a piece."

"The straight life's not agreeing with you."

Kirby shrugged. "Tried it. It didn't take."

"It rarely does," Rothschild said with a knowing look that said he'd seen a lot of men try.

Rothschild reached down into the apron's front pocket and pulled out a folded slip of paper. He slid it face down across the table towards Kirby, motioned for him to take it. Kirby thought about grabbing the handkerchief in his own pocket before he touched Rothschild's meat-and-blood tainted paper, but decided against it, not wanting to offend. He grabbed the paper and started to unfold it.

"Not here," Rothschild said. "You can open it on the way."

"When – wait, tonight?" No need for a performance – Kirby's surprise was genuine.

"I thought you wanted the work."

"I do, it's just – just sudden, that's all." Kirby looked up, projecting confidence. "Yeah. Let's do it. What are we looking for?"

"Not important."

"Wha – how do you expect me to get what you want if I don't even know what I'm looking for?"

Rothschild shrugged. "If you'd let me finish. . ." He paused, waiting to see if Kirby would do just that. "It's not important that *you* know what you're looking for. Your job will be to get in the door. Stevie knows what you will be looking for."

Walk away, Silk, the voice in Kirby's head screamed. *It's never too late until it's too late.*

"Stevie?" his outer voice said instead, pushing forward. "Who the hell is Stevie? I'm not – all due respect, Sir – I work alone."

"Not on this one, you won't."

Quinn had told Kirby to walk away if anything felt wrong, and this was starting to feel all kinds of wrong. Every time Rothschild opened his mouth, he queered the deal a little more.

"I don't know this Stevie character," Kirby said, still trying to salvage things. "And, if I may speak freely, sir, this whole business is starting to make me a little uncomfortable."

"*I* know Stevie," Rothschild said, shaking his head. "That's not enough for you?"

Kirby had to tread carefully here, dangerously close to insulting the integrity of a man who rarely afforded one the opportunity to insult him twice. "Of course it is," he said, backtracking. "Your man's done a lot of this kind of work?"

Rothschild shook his head. "Never."

Walk away. Kirby leaned back in his chair. "Now I'm *really* lost," he said, thinking better of throwing his hands in the air.

"Well, let me give you a map. You don't know Stevie – I don't know *you*. You don't *trust* Stevie – I don't trust *you*. You say you've done this kind of work before – I'm saying Stevie has not. You see what I'm getting at here – as a whole, I'd say it balances out."

This wasn't the way things were supposed to go. Kirby was supposed to make the meet, get the assignment, then hand it over to Quinn and let the Black Bat do his thing. He was never supposed to be involved with the break-in itself.

But the plan was out the window now. He wasn't going to get the target from Rothschild; that much was clear. But he *could* get it from this Stevie character. Go in, find what they're looking for, take it from Stevie, and beat it back to Quinn's house before Rothschild even knew what happened. It wasn't a great plan – but Kirby'd had worse.

The bell over the front door of the deli chimed again. Rothschild, facing the door, looked up and nodded; Kirby looked over his shoulder to see a new player enter the storefront.

"Stevie," Rothschild said.

"Stevie?" Kirby said.

The biggest flaw in Kirby's revised-on-the-fly plan was Stevie; it wasn't going to work if the guy was one of those thick-necked goons with fists the size of boiled hams. But the Stevie that stood before them was the polar opposite: a tall, rangy youngster who could easily pass for a pimply-faced newsboy. The kid was stuffing a chili dog in his mouth as he entered, and mustard dribbled down the front of his shirt. Kirby figured he could handle a guy like this in his sleep.

"You ready to go to work, kid?" Kirby asked, grinning.

But now, as he crouched in a dark hallway outside the law office Rothschild had given them as a target, Kirby was coming to realize his quick assessment of Stevie had overlooked one key factor. The kid had a big mouth on him, and if he didn't shut up soon, Kirby was going to knock him out before he ever found out just what they were looking for.

Kirby felt the slight shift in the pins inside the deadbolt, then threw up a little prayer before he twisted his pick ever so slightly. . . *There.*

They were in.

"About time," Stevie said, brushing past him into the darkened office reception space.

"So what are we looking for again?" Kirby said as he stood; his knees and back stiff with tension.

"Ha – nice try," Stevie said as he walked past the secretary's station towards the inner office door. "If you'd been a little quicker with the lock, we'd have it already and you'd know exactly what it is."

Stevie jiggled the door handle – it didn't budge. "Dammit."

Kirby stood behind the neatly arrayed outer desk, looking at a faded photograph of a handsome older woman he assumed to be the secretary's mother. "Get out of the way," he said, looking up. "I'll get us in there."

Stevie shook his head. "I'm not sticking around here all night – I've got a date as soon as we're done." He lifted a boot and delivered a heavy kick to the doorknob. Another, then another, until the frame splintered and the door swung open.

"Very elegant," Kirby said. "Hopefully the *entire* neighborhood didn't hear that."

Stevie stepped into the inner office, leaving Kirby at the secretary's desk. "Christ," he said as he entered.

"What? This gonna be harder than you. . ." Kirby's voice trailed off as he joined Stevie. The attorney's office had been trashed. File cabinets tipped over, papers all over the floor, trash cans emptied and paintings ripped off the wall. From the open window on the far side of the room, they could hear the relatively quiet Sunday night traffic some ten stories below.

"Not what we were looking for?" Kirby said hopefully.

Stevie stood, speechless for once, scratching his head. "I think somebody beat us to it."

The Black Bat adjusted his binoculars, zooming in on Kirby's face through the open window of the law office. He wished there had been a way to warn Kirby off, get him out of the meeting with Rothschild before things got this far. But things had moved too fast – there just hadn't been enough time.

It had been a busy Sunday afternoon and evening in the Quinn household. Quinn and Kirby had arrived home from the racetrack to find Butch O'Leary waiting impatiently in the study; the big man was eager to fill Quinn in on everything he had learned at Sully's.

"What do you think, Boss?" he asked Quinn once he had finished. "Think it's related?"

"I don't think it's *not* related, my friend."

Kirby related his afternoon at the racetrack, then hurried back to his place to swap suits before his meeting with Rothschild. "I do have standards to uphold," he said as he exited to O'Leary's derision.

And then, not five minutes after Kirby departed, Carol Baldwin, the original member of Quinn's off-the-books support unit in his one-man war on crime, arrived in a breathless hurry. "Three guesses where I've been all day, boys, and the first two don't count."

To Quinn's eyes, Carol remained as beautiful as the first time he laid eyes on her. Of course, the special circumstances surrounding that meeting would color any man's memories. Carol was, in fact, the *first* person Quinn saw after the miracle surgery that restored his sight; never had anything looked as sweet as the face of that small-town girl, hoping against hope that her father's sacrifice – gunned down in the line of police duty – could be turned into something positive.

She had no idea.

"Let's see," Quinn said. "A legal pad tucked under your arm with a file folder. Pencil tucked behind your ear – those say work. Hair pulled back, out of your face. Combined with the dark circles under your eyes, that says a lot of reading."

Carol smiled as he reached for her hands. "And," he said, turning them palms up. "The ink stains on the fingertips look like they've handled a lot of newsprint. So I'm going to say you've been doing some research in the newspaper morgue at the library."

"Very good, Detective," Carol said, laughing.

O'Leary whistled. "That's impressive."

"Not that impressive, Butch," Carol said. "He didn't tell you he asked me to go down there this morning and dig around for him."

"And here I thought that would remain our little secret, Carol," Quinn said as O'Leary shook his head.

"Well, if you're done with your parlor trick, Mr. Quinn, have a seat – I think I cracked it."

Quinn dropped into a high-backed soft leather chair; O'Leary, still a little winded from his morning workout at Sully's, took the couch. "We're all ears, Miss Baldwin."

Carol stood in front of them, doing her best impression of a freshmen-level political science professor. "So, as you know, Anthony, our first thought was that the lawyers being targeted were all former employees of the District Attorney's office who have since gone into private practice." She paused here and pointed at O'Leary. "And that is why you've been sitting outside Tony's office the last few weeks."

"Don't I know it," O'Leary said.

"And we should now take it that that is not the case," Quinn said.

"Right again, counselor."

"So I can take Monday off?" O'Leary asked hopefully.

"I never said that," Carol said. "So my next thought – maybe all the lawyers that were victimized were Jewish. Catholic. Episcopalian. Whatever."

"And?"

"No dice. Eleven lawyers so far – three Catholics, three Jews, a Baptist, a Methodist, a Presbyterian, and a Quaker."

"That's only ten," Quinn said.

"Can't get anything past you, can I?" Carol shook her head. "The third attorney to get hit lists his religion as *socialist*. Which I don't think counts."

"So," Quinn said. "We know how they're *not* related – any idea how they are?"

"You know what I think," O'Leary said. "Maybe they're not. Maybe the guy doing this just hates lawyers."

"You could hardly blame him for that," Carol said.

Quinn winced, a poor approximation of pain, then turned serious once again. "No, they're definitely related. Call it a hunch if you want, Butch, but somehow, someway, I know they are, just like we know Rothschild's connected to all of it. We just have to figure out how – "

"Umm, if you guys would just let me finish. . ." Carol's interruption trailed off into silence.

Quinn made a sweeping, palms-up gesture. "When you're ready, Miss Baldwin," he said. "The floor is yours."

"Thank you," Carol said. She laid the file folder she'd been holding on the table in front of Quinn, open to the documents inside. "All these lawyers – the thing that connects them all. They've all done work for Judge Landis."

"Kennesaw Mountain Landis?"

"The one and the same."

Quinn drummed his fingers on the armrest of the chair, his mind racing. "Eleven New York lawyers, clocking time for a federal judge in Chicago," he said. "That is odd."

"Ah, but you're overlooking a crucial fact," Carol said, clearly enjoying doling this out one piece at a time. "Judge Landis hasn't actually *been* a judge in almost twenty years. And these twelve fellas all did special counsel work for him in the last ten years."

O'Leary nodded, understanding. "As Commissioner of Baseball."

"Winner, winner," Carol said, in a poor staccato imitation of a sideshow barker.

"Wait – you said *twelve*," Quinn said.

"Did I?"

"You did. *These twelve fellas*, you said. There's only been eleven break-ins."

"Is that right?"

Quinn stood up. "Did you happen to find –"

"The address for the twelfth lawyer's office?" Carol ripped a sheet from a legal pad with a dramatic flourish and held it out towards Quinn. "Why, yes I did."

"Excellent work," Quinn said, reaching for the paper.

Carol snatched it back, holding it close against her chest. "What are you going to do with it?" she asked coyly.

"I'm gonna get there first."

And he had.

The Black Bat had slipped into the office an hour or so before Kirby and his new friend had arrived. Armed with at least an *idea* of what Rothschild was after – *baseball* being his working theory – it didn't take long to find something that he imagined could be of great use to a man like Rothschild. So, naturally, he slipped it inside his vest for "safekeeping."

He spent another few minutes looking around for anything of interest, then trashed the office to make the whole thing look like amateur hour. He didn't want Rothschild to think that anything other than random bad luck led to the office being burglarized before his crew got there.

The Bat hadn't expected Rothschild to make his move tonight, though. The plan had been for Kirby to get the assignment from the crime boss, then hand it over to The Bat and disappear for a bit while things played out. But because their move had been tonight, there'd been no time to warn him. And judging from the look on Kirby's young new partner's face, things were not going to end well.

"But Mr. Kirby, look at it from my perspective – it's hard not to think that you set me up."

"How could that even be?" Kirby reached up and wiped the sweat from his brow – a tough task, given the way his hands had been roughly bound together. "I came in, found out about the job – twenty minutes later we're *doing* the job. And I *still* don't know what the hell we were even looking for."

"Make it easy on yourself, Mr. Kirby. Who'd you tip me to?"

Kirby strained against the ropes, felt the hemp bit into his wrists. He had to keep Rothschild talking, keep them from hurting him.

Or worse.

"Are we stealing government secrets here?" Kirby asked. "Nazis? Is that it? Are we working for Hitler?"

"Oh, shut up already." Stevie's voice floated in from somewhere behind Kirby.

"You're still here?" Kirby said, trying to turn around and failing – the rope had him bound too tight to the chair. "Past your bedtime, isn't it?"

Flippant tone notwithstanding, Kirby knew now Stevie was not to be underestimated. No sooner had the two of them returned empty-handed to Schweitzer's Deli, Stevie had clubbed Kirby in the back of the neck with a sap he must have had hidden somewhere in his jacket. No warning, nothing – just a quick blow to the head and Kirby was out cold. The kid may have been young, he may have been thin as a whip, but he fought dirty.

Kirby had to respect that.

When he came to, Kirby found himself bound in the same dining room chair he had sat in a few hours earlier as he met with Rothschild under decidedly different circumstances. This time he and Rothschild sat facing each in the darkened kitchen, the same single bulb overhead providing the only illumination. Somewhere behind him in the dark, Kirby could hear

Stevie pacing around like a caged giraffe.

"Mr. Kirby," Rothschild said softly. "You need to focus on me. I'm the one who will be shaping your future in the next few moments."

Rothschild's sudden change in tone sent an icy finger trailing up Kirby's spine. And when Rothschild walked across the kitchen to the large wooden butcher's block and withdrew an equally large knife, the room grew colder still.

Quinn shoved his legal pad across the desk in disgust, unable to concentrate. He'd been at the office for a couple of hours and had accomplished nothing; he could already tell that this was going to be a wasted Monday.

Kirby had not made it back to the estate the night before. When Quinn last saw him, Kirby and his young partner were leaving the office building in a hurry, and neither man looked pleased. It was obvious from the look at the younger man's face that they hadn't found what they were looking for; Quinn had guessed correctly and took the right file. The question now became just what did Rothschild want with it.

But that would keep for a bit; the more pressing question was just what had happened to Kirby. Quinn found himself staring at the clock on his office wall, counting down the hours until nightfall when The Black Bat could fly again.

"Knock, knock, Counselor."

Quinn looked towards the door, where that deep voice belonged to the burly man now darkening his doorway, Lieutenant McGrath.

"Hello, Lieutenant," Quinn said with a smile. "Didn't see you standing there."

"Well, of course not," McGrath said. "You being *blind* and all."

"I'm sure I don't know what you mean by that, sir," Quinn said, feigning confusion. McGrath had convinced himself that Quinn's blindness was an act, and his attempts to prove it had begun to border on the obsessive. Quinn had personal knowledge that an obsessed man was a dangerous one; as such, he watched himself very carefully around McGrath.

"Didn't mean anything by it," McGrath lied. "Sorry to offend." He dropped himself into one of the two chairs on the opposite side of Quinn's desk. The chair's wooden joints groaned with disapproval. Quinn found himself thankful for the dark glasses he wore; if McGrath could read his eyes right now, he'd know that Quinn had neither the patience nor the time to deal with this visit.

"So," Quinn said, leaning back in his chair. "To what do I owe the honor of this visit?"

McGrath smirked, then scowled. He winked, trying to draw a response. Quinn didn't take the bait. McGrath shrugged, nonplussed.

"Alphons Bennett," McGrath said. "You know him?"

"No," Quinn said, honestly. "Should I? Friend of yours?"

"Goes by 'Rocky' when he's on the street, ripping off wallets, assaulting young women."

"Your friend needs a defense attorney?"

"He's not my friend, and no, he doesn't need a lawyer. All this guy needs is a box and a suit to bury him in." McGrath reached inside his jacket for a photograph, which he spun across the desk at Quinn. "We found him like that last night."

Quinn reached over and picked up the photo, deliberately holding it upside down and backwards. "Like what, Lieutenant?"

McGrath smiled. "Right – I *forgot*." He took the picture out of Quinn's hands, returned it to his jacket. "We found him in an alley down in the theater district, a *bat* carved into his forehead."

"Sounds like he tried ripping off the wrong wallet," Quinn said.

"So you wouldn't know anything about it, then."

"Well, I'm no detective, but that sounds a lot like the work of The Black Bat. Maybe you should find him – ask him about it."

"Yeah, maybe I should." McGrath reached back into his jacket pocket for a pack of cigarettes. "You mind?"

"Mind what, Lieutenant?"

McGrath shook out a smoke, lit it. "Right. I keep forgetting."

Quinn reached across to the other side of his desk, using one finger to push an ashtray from the corner down in front of McGrath.

"Thanks, Councilor." McGrath took a deep drag, then blew a series of smoke rings, watching for Quinn's reaction; he got none. "So, let me ask you another question: Paul Fitzpatrick – friends called him 'Sticky'."

Quinn raised an eyebrow. "Is that a question?"

"The question's the same, smart guy – you know him?"

"The answer's the same, too, *Detective* – no, I don't."

An awkward silence fell over the office. McGrath puffed angrily on his cigarette, filling the room with enough smoke that Quinn's hyper-developed sense of smell made it difficult to remain in the same room. Quinn reached into a small glass bowl on his desk for a hard, tart lemon candy, eager to distract his sensory system with *anything* else.

As he focused on the candy, his mind began to clear. "My turn, Lieutenant," he said pleasantly.

"Turn?"

"A question. What do you hear about Willie Rothschild these days?"

"Willie the Butcher?" McGrath's face narrowed. "What are you up to, Tony?"

Quinn held his hands palms-up in a classic 'not me' gesture. "Oh, it's nothing. Just working some background for a case – Rothschild's name keeps coming up."

"That's not surprising – that guy wets his beak in at least half of everything in this city."

"Everything?"

"Yeah – legal *or* otherwise. If there's money to be made in New York, Rothschild's probably involved somewhere."

"You'd think a legitimate businessman would be wary to do business with someone with his sort of. . . *reputation.*"

"Hmmph. Next legitimate businessman I meet will be the first. Get this – I heard that Rothschild was trying to buy the *Giants.*"

There it was. "Oh, yeah?" Quinn said, willing himself to be as casual as he possibly could under the circumstances.

"I was at a game a couple weeks ago with Commissioner Warner – we were sitting in the mayor's box. Mr. Stoneham came by to chat up the mayor – I overheard him say Rothschild had called him a couple of times about buying the team."

"Guess the Stoneham apple didn't fall far from the tree, does it?" Quinn said. Horace Stoneham had inherited the Giants a few years prior upon his father Charles' death. Charles Stoneham was an inveterate gambler with Tammany Hall ties; he actually acquired the Giants in 1919 in a deal brokered by Arnold Rothstein – the same gambler who would fix the World Series later that year. To find that Willie Rothschild was more than a passing acquaintance of the Stoneham family? Quinn didn't see how anyone would be surprised.

"Like I said," McGrath said, "Rothschild's into *everything.*"

"I can't imagine Judge Landis was too thrilled to hear about that offer," Quinn said.

"Stoneham said it was a pretty fair price he offered, too – but he knows Landis would never approve it."

Quinn nodded in agreement. Landis had been battling gambling and corruption since becoming commissioner of baseball twenty years prior.

It was one thing to have your owners consorting with known gamblers; it was another kettle of fish entirely for one of your owners to actually *be* one.

McGrath stood up to leave. "Well, as much as I'd like to sit here and discuss the trials and tribulations of men more fortunate than we'd ever hope to be – " McGrath paused and took a very pointed look around Quinn's well-appointed office.

"Some of us, anyway," he concluded. McGrath reached across the desk to shake hands goodbye; Quinn made no move to take it.

McGrath chuckled. "You're good, Quinn," he said. "See you in the funny papers."

Quinn sat, listening intently, until he heard the soft click of the door that indicated McGrath had exited the outer office. He waited another minute, just to be sure, then shot out of his chair as if he'd been sitting on a spring. "Butch, get in here!"

He reached across the desk for his legal pad and began scribbling furiously without looking up. "I know what Rothschild is up to – we can end this whole thing tonight. First things first – I need you to head out and find Silk. God only knows where he's gone to ground – if he's holed up with another one of those trampy –"

Quinn stopped mid-sentence, then looked up as he realized he was still alone in the office. "Butch?"

O'Leary came around the corner, walking slowly, carefully, reading from a sheet of paper in his hands as he did so.

"Butch?" Quinn asked again.

"This, uh. . . somebody slipped this under the door when you were in with Lieutenant McGrath. Thought it would be best to wait until he left before I, uh. . . you know, prying eyes and all."

Quinn came around the desk and took the note from O'Leary. "For God's sake, man, what is it, already?"

Quinn scanned the paper quickly, then again. There wasn't much written there, but he slid his dark glasses down the bridge of his nose for an unimpeded third look. The nine words were the same all three times:

I HAVE YOUR MAN
YOU KNOW WHAT I WANT
 - W.R.

Quinn balled the paper up, tossed it onto his desk. "Bring the car around, Butch," he said firmly. "We've got some work to do."

Fact of life: gamblers are weak degenerates.

That simple truth was one Willie Rothschild stumbled upon the hard way a long time ago: his own father was a weak degenerate. Al Rothschild was a drunk and a whoremonger, too, but those vices never bothered his son nearly as much. After all, those were cash-upfront businesses; customers are only spending their own hard- (or otherwise-) earned money. But gamblers? They're spending money they don't yet have, taking a chance that the bill won't ever come due. But the bill always does. Somebody always pays, and as often as not, it's not the gambler; thirteen-year-old Willie quit school to go work at the neighborhood deli to help pay off his father's debts.

And then the bastard up and disappeared anyway.

Young Willie saw no point in returning to school after that, so he stayed on at the deli. He started running numbers out of the delivery door at sixteen; three years later, he took the profits from that enterprise and bought out the Schweitzers. He left their name on the sign, though, the better to draw less attention to the place when he started making book in the back six months later.

The local heavies weren't too happy to see this brash kid moving into their territory; a couple of dead bodies later, a change of heart was evident. By the time he controlled the entire East Side a few years later, the trail of severed thumbs in his wake had cemented "The Butcher" moniker he had acquired. He wheeled and dealed with Tammany Hall; he wined and dined with Rothstein and Luciano.

He was a silent partner in Charles Stoneham's Cuban racetracks; he was there at the Partridge Club when Stoneham won his baseball team in a million-dollar *poker game* with Harry Hempstead. He could have won the club himself if he hadn't folded on an inside straight two hands before.

So when he offered to bail out Horace Stoneham some years later by *buying* the team, a legitimate business proposition to help out an old family friend in need? Who in the *hell* was Kennesaw Mountain Landis to tell him no?

But Rothschild had never believed in rejection; for him it was only temporary, at best. So on the day Stoneham relayed Landis' emphatic answer – "no chance in hell" were the exact words – Rothschild didn't explode. He didn't sulk; he didn't pout. He just nodded, and waited. After all, fortune smiles on those who make their own, or so he'd always heard. And later that very same night, fortune came calling in a major way.

When the bill comes due, men who are out of money start talking. Rothschild learned this, too, at an early age. His father would come home empty-handed on payday, his pockets filled with nothing but stories of 'hot tips' and 'sure things' and 'cold streaks'. The stories were, of course, all lies, but young Willie let him talk.

Even today, he still let them talk. Still mostly lies, but you never knew when somebody might have something interesting to say. Rothschild's life had advanced beyond the point where money still meant something; he had more than he could possibly hope to ever spend. Money was just a means to an end; money bought access, and access bought information. And information bought what Rothschild truly craved.

Power.

So when a down-on-his-luck degenerate in the kitchen of his delicatessen six weeks ago – in the same chair a slumped-over Silk Kirby now sat, he noted – started talking, Rothschild listened.

Turns out that before his life went to seed; Thomas Greene was a high-powered lawyer. He had done a lot of work for a lot of the big players in town; Rothschild knew all of this, had known it before he took the first bet from the guy, but he let him go on.

Greene had even done some work years before with the office of the Commissioner of Baseball; Rothschild knew that, too, but still said nothing. What Rothschild didn't know was just what exactly the man had done for baseball.

Back in 1926, baseball immortals Ty Cobb and Tris Speaker were accused of conspiring to fix a game at the end of the 1919 season. The accusing finger was pointed by another former player. The players involved were all brought before Judge Landis in Chicago for an inquest. Rothschild knew all this; it was widely reported in the papers at the time, as was Landis' ruling: both men were cleared of any charges and immediately reinstated to their respective teams.

Cobb was a man of considerable political connections – he had played poker in the White House with President Harding. Rothschild had known the legendary star socially for years. Cobb was a bitter, vindictive man who had once confided in Rothschild that if he wanted to, he could blow the lid off of baseball in a way that would make the Black Sox scandal of 1919 seem tame. Cobb claimed to have records of owners filing false ticket sales reports with tax authorities, names of owners who scalped World Series tickets; most damning, Cobb had evidence of game fixes – names, dates, you name it. Rothschild had first-hand knowledge of a few of them himself, so he knew Cobb wasn't bluffing.

Greene's claim that he was one of a group of New York lawyers Landis brought to Chicago for the hearing was an odd one, but one that would be easy enough to verify. But the lawyer's final claim was the one that interested Rothschild the most: as a private condition of his reinstatement, Cobb had to turn over to Landis the evidence he had gathered. And what's more, Cobb's file was taken by one of the lawyers and brought back to New York.

When Greene finished his tale, Rothschild fixed him with a long, pregnant stare, then spoke for the first time since Greene's arrival at the deli. "Thank you for that, Mr. Greene," he said. Then he cut off both of Greene's thumbs with a serrated butcher knife.

A visit to Landis with Cobb's file in hand would be more than enough to change the judge's mind; his every decision was predicated on avoiding another scandal, and Cobb had collected enough to launch several. And now, to be so close to the file, and have it taken away, even if only temporarily?

Rothschild reached over and touched Kirby's battered face lightly with the back of his hand. "Mr. Kirby, don't you die on me yet," he said softly. "Where's my file?"

Normally, Rothschild had men on the payroll for this type of work, but this betrayal by Kirby felt somehow personal. Stevie and Patrick were out front, minding the store, so to speak. It was just Rothschild and Kirby, with all the time in the world.

Kirby groaned softly, starting to come around once more. Then he coughed, sending a thin trickle of blood out of his mouth and down his chin. Rothschild stood and moved across the room to grab a whetstone. It was time to get serious.

The overhead bulb flickered, and Rothschild looked up just in time to see it wink out. "Stevie," he called, clearly annoyed. He didn't have time for this. He had changed the bulb himself the night before – must be something with the electric. The light came back on, then out again.

And then on again.

"Patrick!" he called again. "I need you to go out back and – "

Rothschild didn't get a chance to finish his instructions – he was cut off by a pained scream from the dining room, which was followed in short order by the sound of glass shattering. Then more screams, followed by more glass.

Rothschild reached for his knife, as comfortable and familiar at the end of his arm as his hand itself.

It was time to get *very* serious.

Paddy Malone winced as more screams streamed out of the kitchen. Mr. Rothschild and his knives had been back there alone with Kirby for almost twenty-four hours now; every time Kirby fell silent, Malone figured he was finally dead. But Kirby kept rallying, living at least long enough to scream again.

Malone reached up and massaged his temples, his head still pounding from his sparring session the day before. That old has-been O'Leary had dropped him with a lucky shot, and he had felt like garbage the rest of the day. Headaches, dizziness, a little bit of vomiting – all the usual stuff. Playing watchdog was the last thing he felt like doing given the way he felt, but Mr. Rothschild didn't ask. He *said*, and you *did*.

Malone leaned back against the deli counter, then jerked as his arm brushed against the electric slicer. Even unplugged, the thing made him nervous. He opened his eyes and looked to the other side of the delicatessen, where Stevie was enjoying Kirby's screams just a little too much. Malone loved the little guy like a brother, but Stevie was a loudmouth and a creep. They'd grown up together in the same Hell's Kitchen tenement, and Stevie had been the one to introduce him to Mr. Rothschild a few months ago. Rothschild took an interest in his boxing career, and Malone took an interest in some of the side work Rothschild offered. So far, so good – Rothschild had plenty of sporting connections, and Malone figured he was only a few fights away from a title shot. And if Mr. Rothschild needed him for a little heavy lifting done from time to time, Malone figured it for a fair trade.

Stevie jerked a thumb towards the kitchen, where Kirby had fallen silent again. "Think he's dead this time?" he asked. "I hope not – I really want to get back in there and –"

"You're a little creep, you know that?"

"You can go to – What the. . ."

A loud noise outside on the sidewalk cut Stevie short. Yes, this was Manhattan, and a noise outside a restaurant on a relatively busy street should have barely registered – but this one was somehow different. Otherworldly. Unholy.

"What the hell was that?" Stevie asked.

The hair on the back of Malone's neck was standing at full attention. He had no earthly idea what the noise was; he had even less desire to find out.

"Get out there and check that out, Paddy," Stevie said.

"Think we should tell Mr. Rothschild?"

"Tell him what? We heard a *scary noise*? What if it's nothing?"

Malone shook his head. "I don't know what that was – but it ain't *nothing*."

"Probably – but he made it clear he wasn't to be disturbed." Stevie shrugged. "*You* tell him."

Malone looked down at his fingers, instinctively visualizing one of Rothschild's blades sawing through them, one at a time. He shuddered, then sighed. "I'll go check it out," he said.

He stepped out of the deli, then up the steps to the street. Nothing much happening out front; it was a pretty quiet, mostly residential neighborhood, especially on a Monday night after ten. He stood on the sidewalk, hands at the ready, straining in vain to hear anything out of the ordinary. He moved around to the side of the building and went carefully down the alley, still listening. He stopped about thirty feet in and closed his eyes, focusing all of his attention on his hearing. Still nothing.

He opened his eyes – only to find a man dressed entirely in black standing in front of him, his masked face not two inches from Malone's own.

"Boo," the man said, then punched Malone squarely in the chin, breaking his jaw on impact. The pain was both instant and enormous. It even hurt to scream, but Malone couldn't help himself.

Malone dropped to his hands and knees, then scrambled to his feet. He tripped over his own feet as he backpedaled out of the alley, falling again and sending another bolt of pain screaming through his body. He crawled on all fours around the corner, then tumbled down the steps leading down to Schweitzer's.

Another awful sound pierced the air – it took Malone a moment to realize that this one was coming from his own mouth. With great effort, he opened his eyes and found himself staring at a pair of black boots. He cursed his luck as he realized, belatedly, just who was standing over him.

The Black Bat reached down silently and lifted Malone off the ground, no mean feat given that Malone was but a few pounds shy of fighting as a cruiserweight. Malone was powerless to stop him – and just as unable to stop the Bat from tossing him right through the front window of the delicatessen.

There were a number of different ways he could have played this one, but in the end, The Black Bat had decided on the direct approach.

He had been watching the restaurant for the better part of an hour, and felt reasonably confident there were only the two men out in the seating area. He had no idea whether Rothschild was there or not, and he was pretty sure they wouldn't be holding Kirby there. But 371 Wilmont was the one address he had that linked Rothschild to Kirby, so that's where he would start.

The bigger of the two sentries proved fairly easy to dispatch; The Bat lured him outside by sounding a small horn he'd picked up on an African hunting safari a few months prior. By the time The Black Bat sent him crashing through the window, the big man had been effectively removed from the board.

The Bat stopped just long enough to smash the electric box on the restaurant's outer wall, then followed the goon by climbing in through the shattered window – a much more dramatic way to make an entrance than simply using the front door.

The Black Bat wasted none of the time that normal men needed to let their eyes adjust to the darkness – he could see as well in the dark as he could in broad daylight, an unexpected yet very useful side effect of his corneal surgery. He scanned the room quickly in an effort to spot Rothschild's other man, the smaller of the two. He needed to move swiftly while the shock and awe of his assault were still being felt, strengthening his position by taking advantage of criminals' generally cowardly and superstitious nature.

Two more precious seconds elapsed – the Bat needed to find this guy and eliminate him quickly. He turned his thoughts towards probable hiding places and settled on the space behind the meat counter. He took a couple of hard steps in that direction – only to stop in his tracks as he felt something bounce off the back of his head.

He turned to see Rothschild's second man standing there with a heavy sap in his hand. The terror written across the man's face let the Bat know that the blow had certainly been meant to do more than just get his attention.

The Bat had made a number of small modifications to his suit over the last few months. One of them had been to add a tough leather casing to the inside of his cowl; this one had been inspired by a Columbia football game he had attended with O'Leary back in October. The casing had been O'Leary's idea – and a good one.

This nose-to-nose view of the man also clued the Bat in to another fact: this was the same face he had viewed through his high-powered binoculars the night before while monitoring Kirby's failed break-in. This man was Kirby's new partner.

The Black Bat reached out with inhuman quickness and grabbed the man by the throat, lifting him off the ground and slamming the back of his head into the meat counter, shattering yet more glass. "Where's Kirby?" he growled.

The man's face tightened, then purpled as he struggled for air. Blood seeped from the back of his head. "If you ever want to breathe again, you'll tell me where to find your boss."

"Well, Mr. Kirby, would you look at this," a soft voice called from the back of the restaurant. "Your knight in pitch-black armor has arrived."

Kirby had felt wrong from the jump – if nothing else, the last few days had proven that Rothschild's instincts were still good. And when Kirby showed up at the deli Sunday night dropping Sticky Fitzpatrick's name, the warning bells got even louder. Rothschild's man in the police department – another degenerate – had tipped him that Fitzpatrick had been found dead early Saturday morning with a bat carved in his forehead.

Kirby's assignment turned up empty – because someone else beat them to it. So Rothschild took a gamble, even though his lifelong sense of these things told him it was probably a pretty safe bet. He sent a note to Kirby's employer, betting that the three of them were in this together somehow. Quinn. Kirby. And the Black Bat.

Rothschild moved quickly in the back, as Stevie screamed outside. He cut the ropes that bound Kirby to his chair, then dragged his unconscious captive towards the open doorway. Rothschild had a knife in his back pocket, and another, larger knife held at Kirby's throat. The exertion left Rothschild only a bit winded – this kind of thing wasn't as easy as it was ten years ago, but he had kept himself in good shape. He hoped that adrenaline would take care of the rest. "Look at this, Mr. Kirby," he said. "Your knight has arrived."

The Black Bat turned towards him, still holding Stevie by the throat. Rothschild did a quick risk assessment, calculated the odds – judging by his appearance, Stevie had only minutes left on this Earth.

"Let him go, Rothschild."

Rothschild swiped the blade lightly across Kirby's throat, drawing a thin trickle of blood. "Shave and a haircut... two bits..." he sang softly to himself. He looked up, making eye contact with the masked man's dark countenance. Neither man flinched.

"I believe you have something that belongs to me," Rothschild said.

"Let him go." The Black Bat's hands brushed back his cape to expose the twin .45s holstered beneath.

"I'd be careful with those pistols, if I were you," Rothschild said. He nicked Kirby lightly with the knife, opening a second small cut. "Wouldn't want me to *flinch*."

"Fine, go ahead," the Bat said, clearly bluffing. "I don't know the guy."

Rothschild *tsk*-ed, feigning dismay. "Well, that is certainly disappointing. We finally meet, after so long, and you insult me like that. . ."

The Black Bat looked down, as if only now remembering he still held Stevie by the throat at his side. He let Stevie drop to the floor, where he landed, motionless, with a thump not far from where Malone lay.

Rothschild rubbed Kirby's forehead with the flat of the knife. "Aren't you gonna mark your territory?"

"Plenty of time for that later." The Bat stepped towards him. "Maybe I'll use your knife."

"No, sir, that's close enough," Rothschild said, digging the point of the knife back into the side of Kirby's neck. The Black Bat drew to a stop, standing beside one of the small two-top tables.

"If you brought the file with you, go ahead and throw it on that table there," Rothschild said.

"And if I didn't?"

"You did."

Rothschild tensed as the Black Bat reached into the inner lining of his tunic, then relaxed as he produced a letter-sized envelope. "Go ahead and drop it."

The Bat pointed the file at Kirby. "You first."

Rothschild shook his head. "I don't think so. I've heard the stories – this blade on your pal's neck is the only thing keeping you from painting the walls with me."

The Bat shrugged. "We could try it. Maybe you could take me."

Rothschild smiled. "Not even on my best day."

The Black Bat waved the file. "You really think you're going to blackmail your way into buying the Giants? *Really.*"

Rothschild stiffened slightly. This was unexpected. But it shouldn't have been – of course he knew. Quinn must have figured out the angle – they were all working together. Quinn was smart, even for a blind guy,

"Shave and a haircut... two bits..." he sang softly to himself.

and he had connections. He saw the Cobb file, had probably heard that baseball had shot Rothschild down. None of it was exactly secret, if you knew where to look. So of course the Bat knew.

"You're gonna, what? Bet on your own team? Is that how it's gonna play? Maybe bet both sides against the middle, get rich off the vig? Something like that?"

Rothschild frowned. Something about this was starting to feel somehow wrong. Before tonight, he had yet to encounter The Black Bat in the vigilante's year-long war on crime. But he had heard the stories. The Black Bat in the rumors and whispers of the criminal underground was a taciturn killer, equal parts silence and violence. This man was downright glib.

By reputation, The Black Bat was also a master tactician, two steps ahead of everyone else in the game. He was clearly planning something here – Rothschild just couldn't see what.

"I wouldn't expect you to understand," Rothschild said finally.

The Black Bat held the file in his right hand, slapped it against the open palm of his left. "Yeah, I guess not," he said, then flipped the file, spinning it like a pie plate, towards the meat slicer.

Kirby was conscious – The Black Bat was sure of it.

He was pretty sure the first time Rothschild slid his butcher's blade across Kirby's neck, drawing a thin trickle of blood, but not so much as a flinch from Kirby. If Kirby were truly as out of it as he appeared, there would have been at the very least an involuntary twitch. But the fact that there wasn't – Kirby was playing possum, willing himself to be absolutely still.

Then, after the second little cut produced the same result, The Bat was sure.

Kirby was awake and aware, and the Bat was willing to gamble that he was ready and able to lend a helping hand.

Rothschild's eyes widened as he tracked the file's trajectory, ballooning even further as he realized the file was headed for the heavy industrial slicer's blades.

He reached out for the file with his blade hand, and Kirby took the momentary inattentiveness to drop all his weight straight to the floor out of Rothschild's grip.

Rothschild turned his head slightly towards Kirby on the floor, trying to comprehend everything now happening at bewildering speed. The head movement left him slightly off-balance, which Kirby took advantage of by planting a shoe squarely in Rothschild's posterior and giving it a good hard shove.

Rothschild stumbled arms-extended in the same direction he had been reaching – towards the slicer on the counter. The Black Bat dove headfirst in a perpendicular direction, towards the low wall outlet where the slicer's power cord dangled unplugged.

The file and Rothschild's arm reached the blades at the exact same moment as the machine hummed to life.

A horrifying metal scream first filled the room as the slicer's powerful blade meet Rothschild's knife. The machine spit blue sparks all over the deli as metal met metal – and then sucked Rothschild's arm in, all the way to the shoulder, his hand still clutching the knife. The metal scream was quickly overwhelmed by one much more primal, and the flying sparks gave way to splattering blood.

"Knock, knock, Counselor."

Quinn looked up towards the open doorway of his office, where McGrath loomed large. "Lieutenant! Two days in a row – I must be the luckiest boy in the world."

The old beat cop buried deep in McGrath peeked through for just a moment as he slapped a rolled-up magazine against the palm of his left hand a couple of times, then unrolled the magazine and held it out cover-first for Quinn. "You seen this?"

'"I have not – not unless it's a few years old, anyway."

"Right. I keep forgetting." McGrath came into the office and dropped the magazine on Quinn's desk. As it unrolled, Quinn could see that it was actually a comic book.

"You're just going to keep me in suspense?" Quinn asked.

McGrath didn't sit down, choosing instead to stand behind a chair. "It's a comic book – I picked it up at the newsstand across the street."

"A scholar *and* a gentleman – your depth has no bounds."

"You should take that shtick up to the Catskills, Quinn – make a fortune."

"I was thinking radio – take it to the masses."

"Anyway," McGrath said, dropping into the chair. "I thought you might find this story familiar. There's a guy that dresses in all black – suit, cape, mask – and spends his nights fighting crime outside the law."

"It does sound familiar – sounds like a hundred other stories."

"Rich playboy by day – utility belt, the whole thing." McGrath paused. "Calls himself The Batman."

"Interesting." Quinn steepled his hands on the desk in front of him. "I think, Detective, that if you could find the guy who wrote this comic book – I think that you may finally solve the mystery of The Black Bat."

"You think so, huh."

"I also think the whole thing could be nothing more than coincidence."

"Yeah?"

"Not that copyright law's really my thing, but. . . . so you came all this way to show me a comic book, Lt. McGrath?"

"Well, speaking of coincidence, try this one on for size. You were asking me a bunch of questions about Willie Rothschild yesterday."

Quinn frowned. "We spoke about a number of scoundrels yesterday – what about him?"

"Well, just *twelve hours* after you asked all your questions, Rothschild has some sort of horrible late night meat-slicing accident in a delicatessen."

"In a delica – what are you talking about?"

McGrath leaned forward. "Rothschild lost his arm, up to the shoulder. There's another guy with a shattered jaw, and a third guy who's *dead.*"

"What are they saying happened in there?"

"Looks like there was a hell of a fight – but nobody's talking."

"That's too bad."

"You ask me, though. . ." McGrath shrugged. "I'd say the Black Bat happened."

The End

AMERICA'S GAME

Confession: I am a baseball *nerd*.
Not a fan, not an aficianado.
A nerd.

I play it. I coach it. I watch it.

I read it.

When I'm not reading comics, or superhero stories, or crime stories, I like to read baseball histories. This past year, I've read a book about the classic 1912 World Series; one about the Bob Feller – Satchel Paige off-season barnstorming tours in the 1940s; and one about my beloved Big Red Machine of 1975, the greatest team ever assembled. Bar none. No argument. (Unless you think the 1976 Reds were better. I'd entertain that notion.)

Right now, I'm reading a book about Branch Rickey's failed attempt at a third major league in the late '50s, one that would have featured a lot of the revenue-sharing ideas that the NFL would later co-opt to replace baseball as America's Pastime. And after that, I'm going to take a look at Old Hoss Radbourn's amazing 1884 season, in which he won an incredible *fifty-nine* games.

So what does any of this have to do with pulp fiction? Well, let's see. You've got gangsters conspiring with players to fix the World Series. You have the manager of another team partnering up with some of those *very same* gangsters to buy a horsetrack in Cuba. You have teams holding their spring training in Hot Springs, Arkansas, one of the most corrupt, organized-crime heavy cities in the South during the early century. Worried owners hiring private detectives to trail their high-paid superstars once they leave the ballpark to make sure their nocturnal activities are on the up and up. Eddie Waitkiss and Ruth Ann Steinhagen (look it up). Moe Berg.

I could go on. And on and on and on....

And that's just the stuff I *didn't* use in this story. Charles Stoneham *actually did* win the Giants in a poker game with the previous owner. The Cobb/Speaker affair was a real thing – Bill Burgess has done some great research on this, well worth tracking down online if you're interested in some further reading.

And Kenesaw Mountain Landis – his Wikipedia page alone is a fascinating read. If you're into further listening: hunt down a copy of Jonathan Coulton's song "Kenesaw Mountain Landis," which humorously positions the judge as an American folk hero along the lines of John Henry or Pecos Bill (sample lyric: "Kenesaw Mountain Landis was a bad motherf#%^er / He was seventeen feet tall and had a hundred and fifty wives") who saved the game of baseball from the evil Shoeless Joe Jackson ("He always wore his black socks but he never wore no shoes"). It's hilarious and awesome and educational all at the same time.

Boxing and horseracing get the pulp treatment all the time (and, indeed, both figure into my story as well). But, man: gamblers, mobsters, femme fatales, private dicks, spies.... Baseball sounds like manna from pulp heaven. (One more for you: check out the 2011 obituaries for former Mets catcher Greg Goossen some time.)

All the game needed was a masked vigilante to clean it all up.

P.S. I still say the true tragedy of the whole Black Sox scandal was that it tainted what was destined to be (and was, especially once the fix was in) the first World Series title for my beloved Cincinnati Reds. We still fly the banner proudly. We would have won anyway.

FRANK BYRNS - lives and writes in suburban Washington, DC. His short fiction has appeared in such places as *Strange Horizons, Cyber Age Adventures, Everyday Fiction, Powder Burn Flash,* and the *W.W. Norton Anthology of Hint Fiction.* He has previously chronicled the adventures of Jim Anthony, Super-Detective for Airship 27. His third collection of superhero short fiction, *Things to Come,* was released in 2009, joining *Requiem* (2006) and *My Father's Son* (2004); all three are available for order wherever fine books are sold. You can visit him online at www. frankbyrns.com.

BLACK BAT – ROUND TWO

The popularity and success of our first volume of *BLACK BAT MYSTERY* was a genuinely fun surprise. Oh, we here at Airship 27 Productions knew he was a highly popular classic pulp hero. That had been confirmed over the years by the constant reprinting of his original adventures. What we didn't realize was just how hungry you readers were for new adventures of Tony Quinn and his friends. So before anything else, to all of you who picked up a copy of volume one, thank you so very much. Be aware it was your enthusiasm and support that has brought about this second volume you now hold in your hands.

And once again we are just as thrilled with this quartet of stories as we were with the first four. Not only have these four writers turned in terrific action adventures starring pulpdom's nocturnal avenger, but the range of tales is what truly made editing this collection so much fun. Like writer Frank Byrns, I too am a huge baseball fan, and the opportunity to make the world of the grass diamond a backdrop to a pulp story was just wonderful. Then along comes Josh Reynolds with his yarn teaming up the Black Bat with another classic pulp figure, Jim Anthony, the Super Detective. With the publication of his recent Jim Anthony Airship 27 novel, *MARK OF TERROR,* it's easy to see Josh has an affinity for the Super Detective and we always love a good teaming like this. Rounding out the book are stories by veteran scribe Aaron Smith, who, in my humble estimation, has never written a bad pulp tale, and one of the brightest new writers in our field today, Jim Beard.

And if you think the renewed popularity of the Black Bat is confined solely to prose volumes like this one, you are happily mistaken. Radio Archives, those talented audio people from Spokane, Washington, have an audio book adapted from a classic Black Bat adventure. The Black Bat and his cast have also been appearing in various comic titles, most recently last year's *AIRSHIP 27 PRESENTS – ALL STAR PULP COMICS # 1* – which went on to win the Pulp Ark Award for Best Pulp Comic of 2011. Then later this year, Excelsior Comics out of Spain will be publishing a Black Bat comic book anthology which will feature scripts and art from several American creators. Yours truly has an eight-page yarn in there beautiful illustrated by Eric Johns. Do follow my website and we'll keep you posted as to when it is available for sale.

So there you have it, a second-stringer back in the days of his early pulps has finally found the spotlight and rightly taken the center stage of the New Pulp movement. We trust you'll enjoy this volume as much as the first and start bugging us for yet another. Remember, you're the boss and here at Airship 27 Productions, we always aim to please our readers.

Ron Fortier
7/16/2012
Fort Collins, Co.
(www.Airship27.com)
(Airship27@comcast.net)

BLACK BAT MYSTERY

HE OWNS THE NIGHT

One of the most original heroes in all of pulpdom returns in four gun-blazing adventures cram packed with action and adventure. The mysterious *Black Bat* once again patrols the urban jungle, his targets, those who would prey on the weak the helpless. Crusading District Attorney, Anthony Quinn, was scarred and blinded by gangland hoods. When an experimental transplant operation returns his sight, it also grants him the ability to see in the dark! Allowing the public to continue believing he is a harmless, blind attorney, Quinn invents a new identity, that of the crime fighting avenger known as the *Black Bat!* With a trio of loyal aids, he launches his campaign against the forces of evil.

From a giant Nazi-bred monster to a gun-slinging Commie assassin, here are four brand new tales by Andrew Salmon, Aaron Smith, Mark Justice and Frank Schildiner starring the master of the night, the Black Bat, once again thrilling pulp fans with his daring exploits. Long considered the template from which dozen of comic book heroes were inspired, to include Marvel's *Daredevil* and DC's *Batman*, the *Black Bat* is truly one of the most unique characters ever born of the pulps.

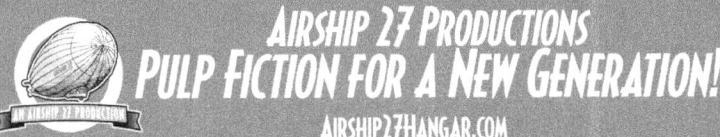

AIRSHIP 27 PRODUCTIONS
PULP FICTION FOR A NEW GENERATION!

AIRSHIP27HANGAR.COM

The Return of Baron Gruner

In 1902 Sir James Damery enlisted the aid of
Sherlock Holmes to prevent the daughter of
an old friend from marrying a womanizing
Austrian named Adelbert Gruner who was
suspected of murdering his first wife.
Dr. Watson chronicled the case as "The
Adventure of the Illustrious Client." By its
conclusion, Gruner's evil intent was exposed
to the young lady when Holmes came into
possession of an album listing his many
amorous conquests. A former prostitute
mistress of the Baron's then took her own
revenge by throwing acid in his face – perma-
nently disfiguring him.

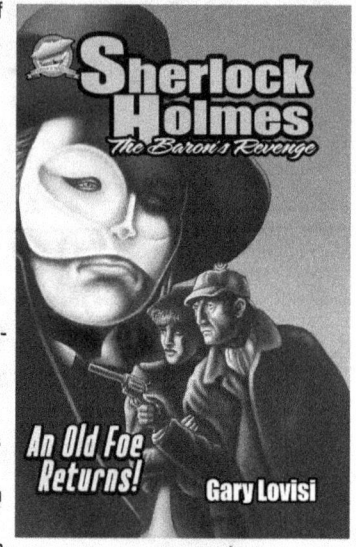

Holmes believed the matter concluded. He is
proven wrong when a hideous murder occurs
rife with evidence indicating the Baron has
returned. Soon the Great Detective will learn
he has been targeted for revenge in a cruel
and sadistic fashion. Not only does the Baron
wish his death but he is obsessed with
causing Holmes emotional suffering. He
desires nothing less that the complete and
utter destruction of the Great Detective in
body and soul.

Gary Lovisi spins a fast paced tale of horror
and intrigue that is both suspenseful and
poignant, all the while remaining true to
Arthur Conan Doyle's original stories. "The
Baron's Revenge" is a thrilling sequel to a
classic Holmes adventure fans will soon be
applauding.

www.ingramcontent.com/pod-product-compliance
Lightning Source LLC
Chambersburg PA
CBHW071240250626
47163CB00001B/262